THE HARDEST THING

THE HARDEST THING

A DAN STAGG MYSTERY

BY JAMES LEAR

CLEiS
PRESS

Published in the United States by Cleis Press, Inc., 2246 Sixth Street, Berkeley, California 94710.

Printed in the United States.
Cover design: Scott Idleman/Blink
Cover photograph: Pali Rao & Jeff Spielman/Getty Images
Author photograph: Copyright © 2013 by James M Barrett.
Text design: Frank Wiedemann
First Edition.
10 9 8 7 6 5 4 3 2 1

Trade paper ISBN: 978-1-57344-929-8
E-book ISBN: 978-1-57344-946-5

The Fight 1

New York City on a dirty night in July is not my favorite place to be. I'd rather be almost anywhere else—I was thinking of the beach in Connecticut or up in the Green Mountains of Vermont, or any of those overseas places I've traveled, most of them warzones, where you can breathe without feeling like someone just threw up on your shoes. But New York is where I am, and short of a miracle New York is where I stay, with temperatures in the 80s and humidity in the 90s and me in my late 30s wondering what the hell happened to my life. A couple of years ago I had a career and a salary, status and respect, and a sense of purpose. Now I'm working nights at a shitty club in the East Village for minimum wage. I don't even have a uniform; the security company is so damn cheap that I have to provide my own. So it's black polyester slacks, a black T-shirt and a pair of black shoes from my dress uniform that I still keep shined—old habits die hard. I look like a burglar, except you can see my face. But nobody looks at my face except to snarl in it or shout in it or, on particularly lively nights, to spit in it. And tonight was one of those nights.

During the week, the Panther Club on East 9th Street is pretty nice by local standards—not too busy, mostly local kids who work in offices by day and fancy themselves hipsters by night, drinking and posing and listening to the deejays or the bands who trot out third-rate art rock and enjoy their fifteen minutes. I don't mind the weeknights: no trouble, easy money, nobody getting too crazy because tomorrow is a working day. It's the Fridays and Saturdays I hate, when the out-of-towners pour into the East Village to feel like freaks for the weekend, and they can't get really freaky without getting really wasted. And that's when I earn my few bucks an hour.

This particular Friday night started like all the others. Quiet till nine, the usual jerks wearing sunglasses in the dark, standing at the bar or smoking on the side-walk, the smoke hanging in the air like fog, collecting under the awning where I have to stand, making my eyes sting and my clothes stink. I hate the smoking laws. Why can't they be allowed to kill themselves inside the club, and let those of us who work outdoors breathe some nice healthy exhaust fumes instead? And then, at two minutes after nine, by some mysterious signal, along came the Assholes. They came up the street in twos and threes, never alone, guys mostly, a few tough-looking girls, all of them with that schoolyard swagger as if they're the kings and queens of the universe and people like me are somewhere down there with the rats and roaches. By nine thirty the club was full, drinks were getting spilled and the atmosphere was turning nasty. A line was forming on the street—it never ceases to amaze me that people will actually wait in line to get into a place like the Panther Club—and you could smell aggression in the air like cheap perfume. Now, I have nothing against aggression. After twelve years in the U.S. Marine Corps, I kind of value it. I like a kid with attitude, if he knows what to do with it. But these guys were just dull drunks with a grudge against life, looking for a fight to perk up Friday night, and if they hadn't started something by the time they got to the door they were more than happy to have a crack at the sap in the polyester slacks.

I don't know where the average out-of-towner thinks that security guys like me are recruited from. Perhaps he thinks we're former schoolteachers or unemployed librarians. The fact is that most of us are ex-military, and that means that we have probably killed more people than he has fucked. I lost count of the number of lives I've taken. Some of them I shot. Some of them fell victim to missiles that I had a hand in firing. But I killed a fair few—twenty, maybe more—with my bare hands. I know exactly how to do it. I can break a neck with the precision of a chiropractor—just a twist and a click and the job's done. So if you're looking for a fight in the East Village on a Friday night, you might want to stay away from the Panther Club.

And this is how the story began.

It was almost eleven o'clock, and the joint was jumping. The line stretched back half a block—New York City must be short of decent clubs these days—and the band was due on, so the suburban tough guys were getting jumpy. Fire regulations mean I can only allow a certain number of people in; as far as I'm concerned they could pack it to the rafters, douse it with gasoline and I'd strike the match, but I have rent to pay. I was standing in the doorway, arms folded and feet planted a yard apart—which, in doorman's language means "stay where you are." I never try to look hostile—it doesn't help—but there's enough of the marine about me to warn off all but the most determined jerk.

And here he was.

Twenty-two, twenty-three years old. Six feet tall, 180 pounds, buzz-cut blond hair, broken nose, wearing jeans that were already ripped when he bought them, a tacky leather jacket and—wouldn't you know it?—a Ramones T-shirt. He was the alpha male in his little dog pack, and he was getting pissed off. His girlfriend was snapping her gum and sulking; she didn't like waiting on the street and thought a real man would whisper in the doorman's ear and sail right on through. So Blondie could either start something, or lose face.

He started something.

"Hey, let us in, man."

"No can do."

"Just fucking let us in."

I said nothing, looked him in the eye. Under different circumstances, I would be very happy to push the little punk to his knees and bury that pretty face in my polyester crotch; the thought was a nice one, and I must have smiled.

"What's so fucking funny, asshole?"

He was a couple of inches taller than me, but I moved my arm a little and let him see the muscle. Come on, cutie, back down, I thought. Let's play nicely.

"What's your problem, dude?"

"Right now," I said, "my problem is you."

"Hey!" That gangster accent was not the one he learned at his Mama's knee. "Don't fuck wit' me, shithead." The blood was rushing to his neck and cheeks. He could talk tough, but he was getting nervous.

"I'll fuck with you any way I like, sir." I kept my voice soft, my breathing controlled. After Kosovo and Helmand Province, the Panther Club isn't such a big challenge.

"Oh, yeah?" He looked around for encouragement. The whole line was watching; this was as good as a warm-up act. "Well, go ahead." He stood right in front of me, bouncing on the balls of his feet. One move—a hand whipped out like a striking snake, a swift rotation, a grinding "click"—and his girlfriend would be a widow before she'd even married.

"Sir," I said, sounding like a robot, "please get back in line. We'll be letting you in soon."

"I don't like your attitude, baldie." His pupils were dilated, the vein in his forehead standing out.

"I'll have to ask you to leave now."

"Fuck off."

Passers-by were stopping, adding to his audience. I stepped forward, close enough to feel the heat from under that tacky leather jacket. It would be a shame to mess him up, but he should know better than to use people's hair-loss issues against them. I've been balding since my midtwenties; all that's left now is a dark band around the back and sides, which I keep clipped.

"Hey, buddy," I said, "why don't you and your friends take a walk?"

"Make me, faggot."

I felt a little fire kindle in my stomach, but I wasn't going to let it show. I maintained eye contact and said, "That's Mister Faggot to you, sir."

Not the most original reply in the world, but it had its effect. Blondie was wrong-footed, and missed his chance for a smart comeback. People in the line—even his friends—were laughing. One of the onlookers, an old lady with long grey hair who I saw walking up and down East 9th Street twenty times a night, cackled like a witch. "Woooooh!" she hooted, shaking her hands above her head like a crazy preacher, "You tell him, honey! Kick his fucking ass!"

I didn't need this. "Ma'am, please don't get involved."

Too late. Blondie, realizing that he'd picked on the wrong bald faggot, found a new target. "I'll kick your fucking ass, bitch," he said, striding out of line toward the old lady. She didn't flinch, but kept cackling.

"Oh, baby," she said, one hand on her hip, the other holding on to her shopping cart, "you wouldn't touch a harmless little old gal like me, now would you?" Her accent was southern, the S's whistling softly through gaps in her teeth.

"Shut up, freak," said Blondie, "I'll break your scrawny fucking neck." His fists were bunched, and he needed to hit something—but again, he'd made a bad choice.

"Oh, yeah?" said the old lady, and before even I realized what she was doing she lifted the shopping trolley by its handle, swung it off the sidewalk and through the air to connect with Blondie's head. Cans of soup and stew rolled out on the street, coming to a halt where

Blondie was now sprawling, blood welling up from a cut on his temple.

Shit. This was all I needed. Grandma was cackling like a hen, dancing around in her worn-out canvas sneakers, tie-dyed skirts billowing out from her legs. Blondie sprang to his feet and pulled his fist back.

Enough. I grabbed his wrist, spun him around on his feet like a ballet dancer, and pushed his arm so far up his back it was just half an inch away from dislocating his shoulder. The breath huffed out of him, and he wriggled for a moment like a fish on a line. "That's enough now," I said, and loosened my grip enough to let him catch his breath. "Time for good little boys to go home."

Now something happened which I hadn't anticipated, which I should have seen coming, and if I hadn't been sidetracked by thoughts of a more pleasant version of this encounter I could have avoided. This kind of lapse in a combat situation costs lives; here, on East 9th Street on a shitty downtown Friday night, it only cost me my job.

Blondie used every last drop of anger and defiance to spin back on the balls of his feet, ducking under my arm as if we were jiving together, and worked up enough momentum to pull his wrist free from my grip. He was fast, I'll give him that—fast enough to take a kickboxer's stance and whip his right leg up in what should have been a very effective roundhouse kick.

But I was faster. I parried his shin with my forearm, moved around and pushed him in the direction his body was already going. Instead of hitting me, he suddenly found himself flying through the air, landing on the street yet again, this time with his leg twisted painfully beneath him and nothing to break his fall. His face whacked straight down onto the concrete.

His girlfriend screamed as if she'd just witnessed a murder, and his friends, four little runts jacked up on beer and bravado, jumped on me. They were easy—one down, two down, the final two grabbed by the collars and squealing as I lifted them off the floor—and all hell breaking loose in the line.

And that's when the manager came out, and called the cops.

I won't bore you with details of the "interview" in his office—my half-assed attempt to say I was only doing my job—and my exit, minus employment, wondering what the fuck I was going to do next. My tiny one-room apartment up on 109th Street wasn't exactly the Ritz Hotel, but it cost about the same.

I left by the emergency exit and had a brief fantasy about blocking the doors and setting a fire—it's so easy to kill hundreds of people, if you know how—and moved on. Another goon in black polyester slacks was out front, another ex-jarhead with scars and muscles and a head full of bad memories. Guys like me are easy to replace.

Great—unemployed, and if I didn't do something about it pretty quick, homeless. Time to read the job ads, pick up the phone and get hustling. So what did I do? I went to a bar. I wanted to get wasted and I wanted to get laid, in that order. I can't remember the last time I had sex sober. Actually I can, and the pain of that memory is one of the reasons I drink.

I'm probably the last man in New York City—hell, in the U.S., probably in the Western world—who still goes out to a bar to find sex. Everyone else is using PCs or smartphones or whatever the hell else, pressing the right buttons to get it delivered straight to their door. Not me; that stuff didn't exist when I joined the marines at the age of 21, and after that everything was provided for me. The world changed—and when I was discharged I felt like Rip Van Winkle, unable to find my way around. I can plan and execute an attack on a terrorist training camp in the deep desert, I can practice ten different flavors of martial arts to lethal standard, but I can barely make a phone call, let alone find someone to suck my dick. So instead of heading home I hit the Downtown Diner, a run-down joint near Union Square where I'd got lucky in the past. It hasn't really been a diner for a long time—if you ask for something to eat, it's always "off tonight"—but they serve beer and spirits and the lights are low, and there are usually a few guys like me—horny and lonely and down on their luck—who are glad for company.

In recent months, the Downtown has been "discovered" by preppies looking for a bit of old-school New York atmosphere; it got written up in a magazine, and for a few weeks the bar was crowded with smart young professionals taking a walk on the wild side. And that's what I wanted tonight: some high-toned civilian with money in his wallet and a taste for rough trade. What could be rougher than an unemployed ex-marine?

I got a beer and made it last, seating myself on a barstool where I was as conspicuous as possible. I might as well have hung out a red light.

Hurry up, dammit, I thought, I'm still sober and don't want to start thinking. I don't want to remember how I got here—step by inevitable step as if someone was pushing me. I don't want to remember the death and the grief and the fallout, the quiet discussions with superior officers sitting at long, polished tables, all of us wearing our medals, all of us talking in circles until they asked and I told and suddenly I was on a plane home with discharge papers in my pocket.

I don't want to remember Will.

And hallelujah, just as I was staring through those wet rings on the bar and seeing Will's face, just as I could feel myself falling into the pit...

"Anyone sitting here?"

Grey suit, dark red tie loosened at the neck, white shirt, collar undone, maybe 27, 28.

"Go ahead."

He got out his wallet—a fancy monogrammed item—and signaled to the barman. "Could I get a beer?"—and then, as if it were a spontaneous after-thought, "Anything for you, man?"

"Sure." I turned to face him, legs apart. "Scotch."

The barman's eyebrow lifted a fraction of an inch as he caught my eye, and that was it. He was generous with his measures when guys like this were paying.

I took a long swig. The whiskey burned my throat.

"Thirsty?" said the guy, sipping his beer from the bottle. I guess he was more used to fancy wine from crystal glasses, but he wanted to fit in.

"It's hot," I said, putting the scotch down before I gulped the lot. I didn't want to frighten him; he had money, and he was just what I wanted: a smooth, handsome yuppie with a gym membership and a condo, drives a BMW up to the coast most weekends, maybe his designer boyfriend's out of town tonight so here he is at the Downtown with an itch that needs scratching...

"Sure is." He ran a finger around his collar. "That's why I needed a beer."

Oh, sure, and you just happened to come into the Downtown Dick Dive to get it. "You work around here?"

"No." He nodded southward. "Financial District."

"Thought so."

"What do you mean?"

I took his lapel between thumb and forefinger. "You kind of stand out in a place like this." I was still wearing my doorman's duds. "Why don't you take the jacket off?"

He did as he was told. His shirt was spotless and tailored to his slim torso. I could imagine what was underneath—one of those perfect, scientifically-designed bodies that you get with an expensive personal trainer. Ten years younger than me at least, and he had it all: money, a career, a future...

I had something he wanted though. It may have been dark in the Downtown Diner, and I may have been wearing black polyester slacks, but he couldn't take his eyes off the prize.

"So what do..." He had to clear his throat, and took a sip of beer. "What do you do?"

"Nothing."

"You mean..."

"I'm unemployed." I looked at my watch. "As of about an hour ago."

"Too bad."

"Yeah. Too bad." I drank more whiskey; there was maybe quarter of an inch left in the glass. He ordered another without asking me. Smart boy. He stuck to his one beer. Even smarter.

The scotch was getting a nice little buzz going. Everything from the neck up was numb, everything from the neck down was tingling, and that was the way I wanted it.

"And what did you do, if you don't mind me asking?"

"Security guard."

"Mmm-hmm..." He sipped his beer and frowned; perhaps that didn't fit his fantasy.

"And before that, I served in the marines for twelve years."

"For real?"

"Wanna see my medals?"

"I'll take your word for it."

I shrugged. "Suit yourself."

"Perhaps I could take you for dinner."

"I'm not hungry." He looked unhappy. "Unless your ass is on the menu." He looked happy.

"Could be." His lips were around that bottle again. Lucky fucking bottle. I grabbed his tie and pulled him toward me, sticking my knee between his legs. Not subtle, but he wasn't looking for conversation.

"Got a place?" he asked.

"Way uptown," I said. We'd go there if he paid the cab fare. Obviously he didn't want me messing up his neutral carpets and suede wallpaper, or whatever guys like him have these days. Perhaps he just didn't want to fuck in the matrimonial home.

"Okay." He scratched his chin; there was enough stubble since this morning's shave to make a crackling noise. I was starting to want him almost as much as he wanted me; I'll never be able to do this for a living, I thought. "How about we get a room?" he asked.

"Serious?"

He shrugged. "Sure. Why not? I don't meet guys like you every day."

Ten minutes later we were in the lobby of an upscale flophouse, or "budget hotel," whichever you prefer; I got the impression that my new friend had used it before. There was a ratty old parlor palm in a beat-up brass pot, a smell of disinfectant and cigarette smoke. The guy on the desk barely looked up as he handed over a key.

"What's your name?"

"Dan." I guess I should have given an alias, but the whiskey was working. "Yours?"

"Scott."

"Okay, Scott." We were halfway up the stairs by now. "You got some condoms in that attaché case?"

"Uh-huh."

"You got plenty?"

"Yeah. Why?" We were at the door.

"Because I'm going to fuck that pretty ass of yours all night long."

Color flushed his cheeks. "Er...okay."

"That's what you want, isn't it?" The key was in the lock.

"Sure. Just...you know. Don't hurt me."

Bit late for that, I thought, as he closed the door behind us. You're the one who picked up the ex-marine in a bar. I grabbed his wrists—I may have been drunk, but I could still move fast—and pinned his hands above his head, pressing them against the tacky brown paint-work of the door. "I'll do whatever I fucking want with you, Scott." I kissed him hard on the mouth. "You're mine now."

And for the next five hours he was.

He didn't just have condoms in his case: he had poppers and a bottle of vodka alongside the files and the iPad. I don't usually touch vodka, but when he passed me the bottle, still wet from his lips, I took a long swig.

And Scott got it all. All the anger that had been building up since that snotty blond brat picked a fight in the line outside the Panther Club, all the frustration of the last two years working in security jobs and living like a bum in a one-room apartment in Harlem, all the shame of losing my job, the grief of losing...someone... I pumped it all up that preppy white ass, and he took it, every inch, every thrust, every smack on the cheeks, every rough word. He took it on his back, with his legs resting on my shoulders or held wide apart in my hands. He took it on all fours, pushing his ass back as I slammed mercilessly into him. He slicked it up with lube and sat on it, sliding up and down like he was on an amusement park ride. I've fucked a lot of ass in my time—it was never in short supply in the USMC, whatever the stupid laws said—but I've never before met a man so happy to have a dick inside him. I swear to god, if I'd had two dicks, he'd have taken them both and wanted more.

I made him come once, jerking himself off as he straddled me, shooting his load over my hairy belly. He climbed off, went to the bathroom to wipe his ass, then he lay back on the bed, threw his legs in the air and steered me in. I made him come again that way, and when I felt his ring tightening around me I started to shoot inside him, coming so damn hard that I saw stars in front of my eyes. It still wasn't enough. He took me to the shower, flushed the condom down the toilet and started sucking me under the hot running water; within fifteen minutes, he was rolling another rubber down my dick and bracing himself against the tiled wall as I skewered him from behind. We watched ourselves in the dirty mirror, saw my thick dark cock pumping into his pale sculpted butt. His personal trainer had done a good job. Between them, they'd created the perfect fucking machine.

Finally, after I'd come twice and he'd come four times, the last time without emission but with the kind of expression on his face that I've only previously seen in field hospitals, we lay side by side on the bed as daylight increased in the sky. It felt good to have someone beside me—another warm body, the chest rising and falling, the intimacy that could feel like love, if you closed your eyes and pretended that he was someone else...someone who cared...

I didn't hear him leave. I didn't wake until someone banged on the door and yelled, "Hey! Housekeeping!" My head was pounding, my eyes felt like broken glass marbles and my guts were griping—too much drink, not enough food.

"All right! Gimme a minute."

Jesus, the room must have stunk like a pigpen, if the pigs drank liquor and used poppers, that is. My dick was hard—I needed to piss—and the thick soft hair around it was sticky with sperm. There was no sign of my new friend, Scott, the man I'd fucked to kingdom come and fallen asleep beside.

I used the bathroom and collected my clothes from around the room.

On the nightstand was forty bucks, two twenties neatly folded under the base of the lamp. Forty lousy bucks. Like I said, I'll never make a hustler.

I stuck it in my pocket and took the bus uptown.

The Job 2

Some Friday night: got into a fight, lost my job, picked up some high-class tail who could have paid my rent for six months out of the loose change in his pocket and woke up with the worst hangover of my life, a sore dick and the grand sum of forty bucks.

I spent Saturday staring at the fly shit on my bedroom ceiling on 109th Street, trying to figure out what the fuck to do with the rest of my life. I could kill myself—nobody would care much. I've got a family, but they're not so keen on their brave boy now that he got dismissed from the marines for inappropriate sexual relations. Who else would notice? A few of the regulars at the smelly little sweatbox I call a gym, the guys who like to watch me in the showers. Maybe the old Puerto Rican lady who lives downstairs and lets me carry her groceries sometimes. That's about it. I can't afford the gym anymore, and if I can't come up with the rent I'll be moving out of 109th Street, and that's it. Dan Stagg has left the building. Hardly anyone knows my name.

That changed on Sunday, when the papers carried a

story about a fight at a nightclub in the East Village in which a psychotic ex-marine had attacked a defenseless college football star, blah, blah, blah. There was my name for all the world to see. "Dan Stagg, 37, who was discharged from the military in 2009." According to "eyewitness reports," I'd picked my victim at random and started beating up on him; the reporter made it sound as if it was only luck that prevented me from having a firearm about my person. Boy, it must have been a slow news weekend if that kind of crap got into the papers. To make matters worse, it got picked up by the radio talk shows—what has New York come to, they asked, when the people who are supposed to be defending our citizens are the ones they need protecting from?

So thank you, Blondie and Company, I am now out of a job, unemployable, and public enemy number one. I wondered if the French Foreign Legion was recruiting, or if anyone wanted a mercenary in, say, Rwanda.

At least nobody got a photograph or published my address, so I can still walk around the streets without being attacked. But that's about all I can do.

I slept late on Monday morning, waking to feel the sun on my body. My mouth was dry and my eyes full of crud, and the hopelessness of my situation weighed so heavy I could barely haul my ass out of bed. I sleep naked, with just a sheet to cover me; the AC in my apartment is an antique window-mounted unit that's so noisy I prefer the heat. So I lay there for a while, watching the bars of sunlight moving across my legs and torso, and I thought about that little prick of a college football star and just what I'd do to him if he was here right now.

Perhaps if I could come, I'd sleep again. I had nothing else to do with my day. No point in looking for a job. Recent experience, Mr. Stagg? Well, sir, just last Friday I nearly killed an innocent member of the public with my bare hands. Thank you and goodbye.

I'd just spat into my palm and was slicking up my dick—it felt good enough to take my mind off the bad stuff—when there was a knock on the door. A knock: an actual physical rapping of knuckles on wood, not a phone call, not a letter, but a personal caller. Two minutes later and I'd have answered the door with cum dripping off my hairy belly; as it was I wrapped a towel around my waist, maneuvered my cock into an unobtrusive two o'clock position, and opened the door a couple of inches.

"Who is it?"

"Dan Stagg?" A man's voice, local accent.

"Who wants him?"

"Ferrari. Enrico Ferrari."

I nearly said *like the car?* but thought better of it. "What do you want, Ferrari?"

"Got a proposition for you."

"Yeah?" He was well dressed in a clean white shirt and charcoal grey pants, thick black hair combed into a perfect side parting. He looked like a movie star. I opened the door a little more.

"Can I come in?" His head tilted enough to see what I was (or wasn't) wearing. "Or you wanna come out?"

"What kind of proposition?"

"A lucrative one." Another inch. "Interested?"

"Come in."

He took in the apartment—the filthy clothes on

the floor, the unmade bed and unwashed cups and plates—and my unwashed body—in one swift glance. "Thanks," he said, nodding.

"Let me get dressed." I picked a grey T-shirt off the back of a chair and pulled it over my head. There were gym shorts at the foot of the bed, and I wriggled them on under the towel. Ferrari watched the performance with a cocked eyebrow. My dick was still half hard, and the thin fabric of the shorts did little to conceal it.

"Okay, Stagg," he said, putting one shiny black shoe on the chair and leaning on his knee. "You're out of work, right?"

"What's that to you?"

"We're looking for someone to do a job for us."

"And who are 'we'?"

"I represent a prominent individual." Was it my imagination, or did he glance at the front of my shorts?

"Yeah, right."

"A very wealthy businessman."

Perhaps Scott had been spreading the word along Wall Street. "Okay, Ferrari, who are you and how did you find me?"

"You're not difficult to find, Mr. Stagg. You're in the newspapers."

"They didn't print my address."

"Your employer...sorry, your *former* employer, was quite happy to provide that." He smiled. "For a price."

"Right." Those bastards at the Panther. "You've got two minutes before I ask you to leave."

"What are you going to do, throw me down the stairs?"

"If that's what you want."

"Okay." He nodded, and looked satisfied. "Tough guy."

"And that's what you're looking for, right?"

"Right."

He had a handsome mug, and my dick wanted to get into it. "So what's the deal?"

"Bodyguard job. Think you can handle that?"

"Depends whose body I'm guarding."

"My client's secretary."

"Oh, yeah?"

"Someone tried to kill him."

"Who tries to kill a secretary?"

He waggled his hand in the air. The nails were neatly trimmed, the back of the hand hairy and tanned. It would look so nice wrapped around my cock. "My client has enemies."

"No shit. Take it to the cops."

"It's a sensitive situation."

"I see." Enough blood was flowing back into my brain to allow me to analyze the situation. "You want me to do something illegal?"

"Let's just say we don't want to involve the authorities at this time."

I shrugged. "Sorry, Ferrari. You got the wrong guy."

"I'm sorry, too." He reached into his jacket pocket and produced a thick brown envelope. "My client hoped that he could count on your cooperation." He slapped the packet against his palm; it sounded heavy. There could be a thousand dollars in there, maybe two. Two grand would answer a lot of the questions I'd been asking myself.

"Why me?"

"You can take care of yourself. And you have a good service record."

"You checked me out?"

"Sure." He smiled. "My client wants a professional."

"Sit down, Ferrari." He sat, carefully hitching up his pants legs to keep them out of the dust.

"We need to get the secretary out of town. Discreetly, understand?"

"I can be discreet." After all those years hiding in the closet, I'm a fucking genius at it.

"But if there's trouble, we need to deal with it."

"Damsel in distress, right?"

Ferrari raised an eyebrow. "The damsel is a dude."

"Can't he look after himself?"

"Have you ever met the children of the rich, Stagg?"

"Enough said."

"You get the first payment straight off, the second when you reach your destination and the rest when you get him back."

"How much?" I was in no position to haggle, but I don't like to seem easy.

"That depends how long you're on the road. And how happy my client is with the service."

"I see." I didn't see at all—who the hell pays someone thousands of dollars to take their rich-kid male "secretary" out of town? "And when do we leave?"

"Tomorrow."

"Suppose I say no?"

Ferrari shrugged. "This city is full of guys like you.

I'm not open to negotiations."

"You have a deal." I put my hand out. Ferrari shook it.

"Good choice." He handed me an envelope. "Here's everything you need to know. You'll see me again."

"I hope so." How about right now, I thought. "And thanks for the job."

"My pleasure, Mr. Stagg." Ferrari stood up straight, adjusted his waistband—he was firm and flat beneath it—and left.

I had a brown envelope in one hand and my dick in the other; it wasn't just the money that interested me about Ferrari. That sharp suit, perfect side parting, smooth-shaven chin, all so neat and groomed—I wanted him.

I pushed the shorts down to my knees, and my dick sprang out, wet at the end.

Ferrari had left his scent behind him—something fresh and clean and lemony, with an undercurrent of wood smoke. God, listen to me—I haven't shot my wad for a couple of days and I'm sounding like a perfume ad.

Maybe he'd turn back on the landing, having "forgotten" something, and find me with my cock out. He'd drop to his knees, not so fussy now about the dust on the carpet; he'd put those big brown hands on my ass, he'd pull me in as he opened his mouth, he'd look up at me with those big brown eyes, and he'd say...

Shit.

I came over the floor where he'd been standing, over the chair where he'd been sitting, shooting as fast and far as a schoolboy.

I wiped my hands on my T-shirt; I'd clear the rest up later. Business first.

I lay back on the bed, shorts around my ankles, my softening cock lying along one hairy thigh, and opened the envelope.

A single sheet of paper, closely printed on both sides, and a small, lightweight key.

Four bundles of notes. Fifties. Fifty in each.

Ten-thousand dollars.

And so, as the July sun blazed through the dirty windows and dried the puddles of jizz, I read my instructions.

An hour later, showered and shaved, I was fitting the key into the lock of a safe-deposit box in a bank on Seventh Avenue. I took the parcel that it contained, signed the book and came straight home on the subway, like any other regular guy running errands around Manhattan.

I had a pretty good idea of what the parcel contained, and I wasn't disappointed: a Glock 19, a nice business-like weapon, with enough ammunition for a small-scale siege. I'm not one of those guys who drool over guns—I can't reel off the features of every single make and model, and I don't have much opinion on different types of bullets—I always thought that kind of stuff was for psychos, or guys who don't get laid enough. But I liked the look and feel of the Glock—a brand new, box-fresh killing machine.

Ferrari and his employer were taking no chances. Nothing to connect them to the weapon.

I sat on the bed, feeling the weight and balance of the weapon in my hand. It was the first time I'd handled a firearm since my discharge, but it felt as natural to me as a brush feels to an artist.

Ten-thousand bucks—the first installment of three. A Glock 19 and a lot of rounds. What was this—a protection job, or a private war?

I re-read the letter that Ferrari had given me. It was as terse and factual as an operational briefing.

> To: Major D Stagg
> Subject: Stirling McMahon
> Objective: Remove subject from present danger in New York City. Subject has been threatened on three occasions and physically attacked by persons unknown. Proceed by road to White Mountains region, New Hampshire, in transport provided. Remain as inconspicuous as possible, report whereabouts daily, await further instructions. Manage and report any hostile activities encountered. Subject's personal safety is of paramount importance. Use all necessary means to secure objective.

In other words, if anyone messes with Stirling McMahon, shoot 'em. Shit, I thought, he must have some damn fine typing speeds. Two possible scenarios presented themselves. One: he's no more of a secretary than I am; he's a prize piece of ass who some wealthy sugar daddy wants off the scene for a while, for whatever reason. Two: he poses a threat to someone's business operations, deliberately or otherwise. If the former, why not just send him off on a Mediterranean cruise? If the latter, the kid would have to be a damn fool to hit the road with a mean-looking motherfucker like Major D Stagg. They knew how to flatter me, that's for sure—but they also wanted what only the USMC could give them. Absolute security.

The letter ended with an itinerary. Rendezvous 1100 Tuesday at Penn Station where subject would be handed over. Bring minimum luggage. Proceed by foot to car rental on 37th and 8th, where a vehicle was booked in my name. Transport subject north out of town, avoiding main roads and toll booths, heading toward New Hampshire. Journey to take three days, staying overnights in motels of my choice, as cheap and anonymous as possible. Arrive in vicinity of White Mountain National Forest on Saturday, book into motel and await further instructions, pending ultimate return of subject to New York City "or alternative destination." Enclosed in the envelope was a brand-new cell phone.

"Welcome to the twenty-first century, Stagg," I said to myself. A cell phone, a weapon and ten grand; hey, what was to stop me from setting off to Vegas, buying the best ass the city could provide and either drinking myself to death or blowing my brains out?

That good old Marine Corps training, that's what— and the instinctive delight in a mission. For the first time since landing on American soil I felt like I had a purpose in life. I wouldn't let them down. Maybe, if things went well, I might get another job. Might start dressing in smart suits like Enrico Ferrari, might even taste a piece of that prime Italian sausage. Okay, it was likely to be on the wrong side of the law—but look where playing by the rules had got me. Twelve years of impeccable service, until they asked and I told. Fuck that. Fuck any idea of going back to the military now that they'd changed the rules of engagement. It was enough for me that they threw me out once; I wasn't going to give them a second chance. I'd been one of the good guys all my life, wherever my country needed me most. To hell with duty. Now I was looking after number one.

Or so I thought.

At the end of the itinerary, in block capitals, the words

MAXIMUM SECURITY OPERATION
ABSOLUTE SECRECY AT ALL TIMES PARAMOUNT.

Not a problem. When you've lived your entire adult life in a state of absolute secrecy, it's second nature. You don't think in terms of "truth" and "lies." You think about expediency, operational security, all the bullshit that they used to justify the fact that they didn't like queers. And I lapped it up. From school to the Naval Academy and into the Corps at the age of 21, I never had to think for myself. I followed orders, I did what I was told to do and I thought what I was told to think. I was as efficient as that weapon lying in my lap—each part carefully designed by its makers to do a specific job. A gun is used for killing and wounding; if you want sweet music, get a clarinet. Dan Stagg was the same: a well-oiled machine with no ideas about right and wrong, good and evil. Black was black, white was white and I was not much interested in grey. There was plenty of ass to be had, both military and civilian, for the Few and the Proud. I was just one of the guys—one of the many, many guys—who "didn't have time for chicks," "didn't want to get involved"; sex with men was just good clean fun, an extension of what we did in the gym and on the sports field. If someone had called me queer, I'd have busted their chops.

And then I met Will.

Will was not part of the plan.

I was meant to keep rising through the ranks, touring the world's combat zones, killing people for the greater good, fucking asses and mouths and sucking the occasional cock if I was drunk enough—and then retire and spend my pension on hustlers. Maybe raise horses. Or just shoot myself. Fuck knows.

What I was not meant to do was fall in love.

We met in 2006. I was 31, Will was 25, I was a captain, he was a corporal, and we were stationed in Iraq, trying to "keep the peace" in the aftermath of Fallujah. It was a shitty posting, and even officers like me, brainwashed since high school, wondered what the fuck we were doing there. The locals hated our guts, other military personnel in the region resented us, and we wanted to get out ASAP. Our days were spent on pointless patrols of the ruined suburbs. Our nights too often ended in fights. I spent more time dealing with internal disciplinary issues than I did with insurgents— what was left of them.

Will Laurence was just another sullen young marine who'd been causing trouble around the camp, getting into fights—and now he'd whacked a gunnery sergeant so hard he'd dislocated the guy's jaw.

Will stood in front of my desk like a thousand kids before him, arms by his sides, head up, shoulders back, staring at a spot on the wall somewhere above my head. Sure, he was cute—brown hair, big blue eyes, narrow waist—but when you've served in the marines for as long as I had, you stop noticing. You're surrounded by candy all day, every day. Sometimes it's hard to ignore—when they're playing volleyball stripped to the waist, or in the showers, horsing around with soap and water—but for the most part, I could look at all that beauty without turning a hair.

"So, Corporal Laurence."

"Sir."

"Fighting." I sighed. "Anything to say?"

"No, sir."

"Looks like you got a beating." He was grazed on his left cheekbone, and the skin around the eye was discolored. I knew from the report that the other guy came off a lot worse.

"Yes, sir."

"And I believe you struck a superior. Sergeant Hall."

"Yes, sir."

"That's a serious offence, Corporal."

He blushed, but said nothing. Good boy. Observing the code. Settle things like men. Don't go whining to the officers.

"Well, Corporal Laurence, I'm looking at your service record, and it seems like you're a pretty good marine."

"Sir."

"So you must have had a reason for fucking up like this."

No response, eyes fixed on the wall, high color in his

face, a little sweat on the temples. He was starting to look more interesting to me. Break down the bravado of these boys, get them on the wrong foot when they're faced with authority, and the fun begins.

"Seems a shame, when you're up for promotion, Will."

He glanced down, surprised by the familiarity. I smiled.

"What's the story, then? Come on. Tell me. Oh, for god's sake—at ease, corporal."

He relaxed his spine, dropped his shoulders and moved his feet apart. "It's nothing, sir, honestly."

"I'm not asking you to squeal, Will. I just want to know why you'd mix it with an asshole like Sergeant Hall."

That got him, and he looked me straight in the eye. "Sir?"

"I know all about Hall. He's a meathead and a retard, and he only made it to the rank of Gunnery Sergeant because he's useful in combat. The rest of the time, he's a dick."

Will's mouth twitched into a smile. "He sure is." When he wasn't barking his responses in the approved jarhead style, he had a slow, lazy accent—Tennessee, maybe, or South Carolina.

"And has he been giving you a hard time?"

"Nothing I can't handle, sir."

"So I see. You busted his jaw."

"Dislocated it, sir."

"Very considerate of you."

"I was thinking of the medics, sir. Didn't want to inconvenience them."

He held my gaze for five seconds, and then we both started laughing.

"Okay, Will. Sit down." He obeyed. "Now listen to me. I've got enough on my plate without having to make this into a disciplinary matter. If you tell me that Hall was giving you a hard time, I'll just put this down to youthful high spirits, okay? I don't like bullying, and I guess that's what he was doing."

Will said nothing, but his gaze was clear and steady.

"And I guess he was abusive and threatening and so on. Correct me if I'm wrong."

"You're right, sir."

"Just out of curiosity, what did he say?"

"He called me a queer, sir."

"Ah." We had skated on to thin ice. A few careless words was all it would take to get us both into deep water. He knew it, and I knew it.

Don't ask, don't tell.

"Okay, Corporal Laurence," I said, tidying his papers and trying to sound like a captain of the U.S. Marine Corps rather than a nervous teenager hoping for a first date, "I think we can close the file on this one. Just keep away from Hall and his boys in future."

"I'll do my best, sir."

He was still sitting on the other side of the desk; damn, he suddenly looked hot to me, and I wanted him badly. Right now. Over the desk, if necessary.

"That's all, Corporal."

He stood up and saluted. "Yes, sir. Thank you, sir." But now he wasn't staring at the wall. He was looking into my eyes, and I was the one who was sweating.

Shit. Memories. I waved my hand around my eyes, as if I was brushing away flies. Damn it, I don't need this now. Memories of Will.

I have a job to do, I have ten grand in my hands; I have a gun and an itinerary. I don't need principles. I tried principles. I tried letting my guard down, and look where it got me. Will, and all that followed.

I'm not going down that road.

I stood up, and felt the weight of the Glock in my hand. Good and heavy. Well balanced. Cool and precise. Engineered.

I looked at my watch: nearly 1900hrs. Time to eat, pack a bag and get some sleep. A new operation begins in the morning. A step into the unknown, at Penn Station. Goodbye, 109th Street, hello New Hampshire, the open road, cheap motels, fresh air and mountains and the Subject.

Stirling McMahon, a snot-nosed brat that I'm being paid thirty thousand to babysit.

I put the gun under the mattress and stripped off for the shower. My cock was hard from thoughts of Will Laurence—but that was over. Over, forgotten, dead.

Time to start thinking about the future. And, for the first time in over a year, I began to feel as if I might actually have one.

Ferrari was easy to spot, even in a busy place like Penn Station. Immaculately dressed despite the heat, hair combed into that precise side parting, he looked as fresh and fragrant as an aftershave ad. I was wearing an old green T-shirt and a pair of chinos, sweating like a pig after riding the subway downtown.

"Good morning, Major Stagg." He checked his watch, an elegant gold bracelet against tanned wrists. "You're very punctual."

I shrugged. Of course I'm fucking punctual. "Where's the passenger?"

"In the bathroom." There was an edge of irritation in Ferrari's voice. "For the fifteenth time since we got here."

"What's he doing?"

"He's nervous."

Yeah, right. That's why people hang out in railway station toilets. "If he has diarrhea, he's going to have to stick a cork in it. I'm not stopping at every restroom between here and New Hampshire."

"Relax, Stagg. He won't give you any trouble." Ferrari scanned the crowd, thinning now that the morning rush was over. "Here he comes." I followed his gaze, half expecting to see a fat geek with glasses and an Eminem T-shirt.

Wrong.

He was six feet tall, with blond hair that just happened to catch a stray ray of sunlight. It flopped down over his forehead so precisely that he looked as if he'd come straight from the hairdresser's. Maybe that's what he was doing in the john—fixing his hair. Half his face was concealed by oversize aviator shades, the lenses fading down from dark brown to pale orange, the frames gold. He was wearing a sleeveless T-shirt that stopped just below his belly button, and denim cut-offs riding low on his hips, with several inches of brown stomach and white underpants between the two. The look was completed by a pair of expensive-looking sandals.

He stopped, rested his weight on one foot and put his shades on top of his head, holding the hair out of his eyes.

"Oh," he said. It was the sort of "oh" you might use if you'd stepped in dog shit.

"Dan Stagg," said Ferrari. "Stirling McMahon."

I extended my hand; he didn't take it, but slurped instead on some fancy coffee concoction in a plastic beaker with a straw.

"Shake the man's hand, Stirling."

He rolled his eyes like a kid who's been ordered to tidy his room, and extended one soft, smooth paw in my direction. I took it and squeezed, tempted to break a couple of little bones just to show who's boss. I began to realize why this job came with such a high price tag. He stared into space and sucked on his drink.

"Okay, Stagg," said Ferrari. "You've got everything you need, right?"

"Sure."

"And remember—absolute secrecy and security."

"Got it."

"You report your whereabouts at least once a day."

"I understand, Ferrari. I can read. Now I have a question for you."

"My client does not..."

"Why New Hampshire? Why's he safer up there than anywhere else?"

"If you can't handle the job, Stagg..."

"I'm not saying that. But if you want me to do it properly, I need to be in the picture. What's so special about the White Mountains?"

"I hate the mountains," Stirling said in a flat voice, a simple statement of fact. Ferrari and I ignored him.

"The destination is immaterial," said Ferrari. "It's quiet and it's out of town, that's all. Anyone looking for him—well, needle in a haystack. My client has no connections with the area. It's not near any major commercial centers."

"In other words, you chose it at random."

"There were other considerations, but..." Ferrari waggled his hand in the air. "If that's what you want to think, yeah. Happy?"

"With the money you're paying me, I'm fucking ecstatic."

He smiled. "Good." I wished it was Ferrari coming

on this road trip with me, not the living Ken doll with the overpriced coffee.

Stirling was wandering off. "Hey!" It wasn't a friendly hey—it was a short, loud, marine-officer "hey," barked and startling. He stopped. "Just where do you think you're going?"

"The bathroom." He drawled it, whined it, trying to provoke me. I grabbed his upper arm and he dropped his coffee, sticky brown liquid spilling out over the station floor. "Aaagh!" he screamed. "My sandals!"

Ferrari laughed. "Okay, Stagg, he's all yours. Happy holidays!" He melted into the crowd; when I looked for him, he'd disappeared. I had one pissed off blond brat on my hands.

"What the fuck do you think you're doing, asshole?" he said. "Let me go."

I kept squeezing his bicep and steered him briskly out of the station. He was so surprised that he said nothing. When one of his shoes fell off, he stumbled and almost fell; I righted him, picked up the shoe and kept going. By the time we reached the street his face was so dark with anger that you could see it through the sunbed tan and tinted moisturizer.

"When my boss hears about this…"

"Shut the fuck up." Might as well get started on the right foot. "You don't speak until we're in the car. Got it?"

He took a deep breath. I knew exactly what he was planning: start screaming, cause a commotion, slip away. I acted quickly: put an arm around his shoulders, drew him in and delivered a swift jab to the solar plexus. He was only slightly winded—enough to stop him from screaming, not enough to prevent him from walking.

We were two blocks uptown before he recovered enough to stand up straight. But at least he wasn't talking anymore. We made it to the car rental place without further incident. I left him outside—if he'd been a dog, I'd have chained him to a lamp post, but had to content myself with threats. When I came out with the car keys, he was rubbing moisturizer into his hands. Fucking moisturizer, for god's sake. I was grinding my teeth. Jesus, Stagg, control yourself. You've been on this job for half an hour. Let's have a little professionalism. I took a deep breath.

"Okay, Mr. McMahon?"

He pouted and said, "No," as if explaining to an idiot.

"Let's hit the road, then." He didn't move. "Shall I carry your bag?" Like me, he had what the airlines call one item of hand luggage, only his was covered in logos and buckles and straps, and mine was a grungy old knapsack that still contained a few grains of Afghan sand.

Stirling said nothing, just kept rubbing that scented goop into his hands.

"Right." I picked up his bag and hefted it over my shoulder. "The car's in the basement garage." He didn't move. "After you," I said. I held open the door that led down to the garage. "Go ahead."

If ever a manner of walking could express contempt, that was how Stirling McMahon descended the stairs to that dingy underground garage on 37th Street. He crossed his feet over each other with each step, shaking his ass in my face. Oh, he was going to get such a spanking. Maybe that's what he wanted. Maybe he likes to wind guys like me up to the point where we lose our cool and knock him about a bit. Spoiled brat like that—probably needs it rough. I wondered if he'd done the same to Ferrari, and if Mr. Neat-Suit-and-Side-Parting had lost his cool and tanned the kid's hide.

Nice thought. I'd be happy to help him. One of us at each end.

Okay, I couldn't let thoughts of sex distract me from the job. After being fired from the Panther Club, I couldn't afford to fuck up again. With thirty grand in the bank I could start over, put the past behind me, forget Will, forget what happened in Afghanistan, forget the U.S. Marine Corps...

Stirling's ass kept swinging. Well, we had a long trip ahead of us, a lot of nights in cheap motels, and if fucking him turned out to be part of the job, I'd endeavor to give satisfaction. Never let it be said that Major Daniel Stagg refused a challenge.

Stirling sulked all the way out of town, sitting in the backseat of the car with his shades on, fiddling with his nails, sorting through the contents of his bag and even at one point fixing his hair in a little hand mirror. Every so often he sighed and tutted. He didn't speak until we were well on the way to Poughkeepsie.

"Gimme your phone."

"No."

"I need to make a call."

"Sorry."

"I said I need to make a call."

"And I said no." This was part of the agreement—no access to phones, nothing that would reveal our location.

Left to his own devices Stirling would have been texting, chatting and tweeting his whereabouts to anyone that cared to listen. Deprived of a phone he quickly ran out of things to do. He filed and polished his nails, brushed his hair, moisturized his hands about twenty times and pulled up his T-shirt to examine his abdominal muscles in detail; from what I could glimpse in the rearview mirror, they were nothing to be ashamed of.

In the end he got bored.

"You're a lousy driver," he said when a truck cut me off, overtaking us on the inside at about 80 mph.

"Thanks."

"You almost got me killed."

"I'll try harder next time."

"You're only doing this because my boss is paying you."

"Correct."

"Why haven't you got a proper job?"

"Guess I'm not as smart as you."

He shut up for ten minutes and shifted around on the backseat, trying various positions—feet up to the left, feet up to the right, feet tucked under him. Finally he attempted to hook his legs over the back of the passenger seat. I swatted them down.

"Hey! That's dangerous!"

"Don't fucking touch me, man." From the way he yelped, you'd think I'd just slapped him in the face.

"Sit still and shut up. Let me drive."

More tutting and sighing, more rearranging of limbs and clothes. Every new position revealed more flesh.

We approached Poughkeepsie and crossed the river, sticking to the quiet roads. Countryside replaced the urban sprawl, and the air was noticeably cooler. I wound the window down.

"Hey! Close that."

"No."

"It's messing up my hair." I had no reply for that. "It's okay for you. You're bald." He made it sound like an accusation.

I ran a hand over the top of my head. "Yes. I'm bald."

"How old are you?"

"Old enough to be your father."

He leaned forward, resting his arms on the back of my seat; I could feel his breath on my neck. "I don't think so. My father's ancient."

"Comes to us all."

"So come on. How old are you?"

On the whole I preferred petulant silence to this taunting interrogation, but perhaps it would pass the time. "I'm thirty seven."

He said, "Ha!" as if he'd just scored a major victory, and said, "That's so old, that's like nearly forty."

"Indeed it is."

"And you're still driving cars for a living."

"Looks that way."

He picked a bit of thread off the shoulder of my T-shirt. "Didn't you ever think of doing anything worthwhile?"

"Don't you think this is worthwhile?"

"You know what I mean. Having a career."

"I had a career." Shit—I hadn't meant to tell him anything about myself.

"Oh, yeah?" His tone was jeering. "What?"

"What do you think?"

He sniggered through his nose. "Street sweeper? Janitor?"

"You got it."

"No, go on. Tell me."

"Why are you so interested all of a sudden?"

"I'm bored." He reached out and touched the top of my head. I waved him away.

"Quit that."

He giggled. "Baldie."

"Just shut up, McMahon. Go to sleep or something."

He threw himself back into his seat, pulled his T-shirt up and rubbed his stomach. "I'm not sleepy." He caught my eye in the mirror. "I'm hungry."

"Okay. We'll stop soon." It was after one o'clock, and my stomach was rumbling, too. I need regular feeding, three times a day, plenty of protein, or I get nasty.

"Where are we sleeping tonight?"

"Nowhere fancy, I can tell you that."

"Where?" He crooked a leg and pushed his crotch forward. He knew exactly what he was doing.

"Depends how far we get."

"I want somewhere with a pool." He stretched his arms, somehow managing to make his shirt ride up over his tits. "I want to swim."

"You'll be lucky if it has a shower," I said, but in truth the thought of Stirling McMahon splashing around in a pair of Speedos was kind of interesting, however much of a brat he was, however much he filed his nails and primped his hair.

Another truck swerved in front of me, horn blaring,

and I had to jab the brakes to avoid a collision. Shit! My concentration was going to pieces. Stop thinking about ass, Stagg. Focus on the job. Deliver the result. Get laid when this is over—and if you need to, jerk off in the shower.

Stirling laughed, lay back and closed his eyes. For the next hour we drove in silence. I don't know whether he slept, but at least he was quiet.

Hunger made me stop. We were getting into the Catskills, giving Albany a wide berth, and I knew that if we didn't get something to eat soon we'd run out of options. Fresh air and pretty scenery are fine and dandy, but they don't fill your stomach.

We passed through a small tourist town, one of those places with a row of motels and tacky souvenir shops. There was a supermarket on one side of the street, a coffee shop on the other—that would do. I parked, wound up the windows and left my passenger snoozing in the back. If he tried to make a run for it, he wouldn't get far—but I took the precaution of locking the doors.

I got bread, ham, tomatoes, cheese and apples in the supermarket, and two coffees from the coffee shop.

"I need the bathroom," Stirling said when I got back in the car. "Let me go into one of those motels or something."

"No can do. We're going to have a picnic. You can go pee-pee in the woods."

"I need to do number two."

"Then we'll dig a little hole." I pulled away from the curb. "Just watch out for poison ivy on your ass."

I found a quiet spot in the woods with a picnic table

and a view, just the sort of place that a honeymooning couple might stop. And that's probably what we looked like—New York newlyweds screwing each other's brains out in cutesy motels before heading back to their designer condo in Chelsea. Well, if that's what people wanted to think, fine. As long as we didn't look like a professional bodyguard and a rich kid with a price on his head, it was all good.

We ate in silence. When Stirling wasn't making an effort to be obnoxious, we got along just fine. Stuffing his mouth with bread and ham, swigging his coffee, chewing and swallowing, he seemed like a regular guy. A decent haircut and a good scrub to get the crap off his face and he'd be...

"I want to swim."

There was a fair-sized pond beyond the trees, surrounded by boulders that gave easy access to deep, clean water. The idea of a dip after hours on the road was attractive.

"No." I balled up the paper bags and swept the crumbs on to the pine needles; the ants could have 'em. "Time to get going."

"What's the big hurry?" He'd already stripped off his shirt; his skin was golden and smooth. "We don't have to be anywhere in particular, do we?"

He was right, of course. "We need to keep moving."

He kicked off his sandals and unbuttoned his shorts. "I don't see why. There's nobody here to see us." His shorts dropped to the pine needles, and he stepped out of them. All that was left was dazzling white briefs, skin tight.

"Because I say so."

He shrugged, and started tugging at the waistband of his underpants.

"Okay, that's enough. If you want to swim, go ahead, but keep those on."

"Why?"

"Because I don't want us getting arrested. We're supposed to be staying out of trouble."

"Whatever." He let the elastic ping back against his hips and walked on the balls of his feet over to the rocks. He clambered over, there was a splash and he disappeared.

Letting him out of my sight was not a good idea—and he was right, there was no particular timetable. The water sure looked inviting. It was a long time since I took my last shower at 109th Street—and even longer since I swam in open water.

When? With Will, maybe?

Did we ever go swimming together?

Of course. A brief flash of moonlight on water, Will's shoulders breaking the black surface of the sea, brown arms and legs moving in slow circles, our mouths joining, wet and salty...

Forget that. I screwed up my eyes, shook my head to erase the memory.

Well, what the hell. I have to keep an eye on him, and it won't do me any harm to freshen up. I stripped down to my shorts and followed Stirling into the water.

He was floating on his back. I might as well have saved my breath—his underpants had turned transparent. I muttered, "Jesus," and slipped in. The water was cold but good.

I swam out for a hundred yards, then turned in a

big loop. Stirling was still floating, his head back, hair streaming out. His eyes were closed, and the sun sparkled on his wet body.

I was getting a hard-on. That would have to be got rid of before I got out. For all I knew, this Lolita act was just another way of winding me up; if I laid a finger on him, let alone what was rising in my shorts, he'd scream rape and the game would be over. Another report in the papers, perhaps a spell in jail, and further unemployment.

I thought about Mom and Grandma and amputations and dead kids—I'm never at a loss for things to make unwanted erections go away.

When it was safe, I said, "Okay, Water Baby, you've had your swim. Let's go."

We climbed out over the boulders. It could have been an accident, but when Stirling's foot slipped I got a face full of wet, white cotton ass. I pushed him forward. It felt like a basketball.

And then, as we stood dripping on the pine needles, he peeled his underpants down with no attempt to turn away from me. Damn, he was nicely put together. Everything in proportion. Nothing too big, nothing too small.

Mom. Grandma. Amputations. Maggot-infested wounds.

He started drying himself with his T-shirt, dabbing and wiping, turning this way and that. I stepped quickly out of my shorts, kicked them toward the car and struggled into my chinos. My legs were wet, a foot got caught in the fabric and I stumbled, nearly fell. In righting myself I turned full on toward Stirling, his shorts unbuttoned, golden fuzz climbing from his crotch up to his belly button, his damp shirt bunched up in his hand.

"Careful, Mr. Stagg," he said. "Take your time." He buttoned his shorts while I disentangled myself. My feet were covered in dirt and pine needles. "Need a hand?"

"I'll manage." If he'd decided at that point to drop to his knees, I wouldn't have stopped him. We were only separated from the road by a few trees; anyone could have driven in and seen us, but for a second I didn't care. Stirling said nothing and watched me struggle into my clothes. By the time I was dressed—chinos over my bare ass—I was pretty much fully hard. I moved around the car and got into the driver's seat.

This time, he took the passenger seat.

"Don't forget to buckle up," he said. He pulled the seatbelt across his chest; I saw the strap sinking into his silky golden skin. My cock ached. If we'd both been marines, getting into a vehicle after a spot of skinny dipping, I'd have had no hesitation about getting it out, with one of the usual lines—*hey, how about giving a buddy a hand? Shit, I wish we had a couple of chicks with us right now.* The traditional excuses.

But now I felt awkward and angry. I started the car, revved the engine and sent pine needles and dirt flying as I sped out of the woods and back to the open road.

We were close to Utica by late afternoon, taking a long loop away from our final destination, figuring that I needed to kill time; the plan was to arrive in the White Mountains by Friday. That left two full days on the road, and we might as well take the scenic route.

Stirling slept for a few hours, head resting on his bent arm. The hair in his armpits was pale and damp. Now that he'd washed some of the toiletries off his body, he gave out a nice scent of warm flesh.

Around five o'clock we reached Richfield Springs, a little town with no outstanding features. I found a motel and rented a room from the old guy in the office; I don't think he even looked me in the face.

The room could have been anywhere in the United States. Two huge beds with floral covers, a ceiling fan, fancy glass lampshades and a tiny bathroom separated from the sleeping quarters by a folding door in brown wood-look plastic. The perfect, anonymous, cheap motel. Ferrari could not have wished for a better choice. A couple of cars were parked outside other rooms, but there was nobody around the parking area apart from an elderly German shepherd sitting in the shade of a dirty red pickup truck.

Once we were inside, we were invisible.

"Where the fuck is this?" said Stirling, looking around as if I'd pushed him into a completely alien environment.

"Richfield Springs, New York. The Happy Highway Motel. Room number four, to be precise."

"It stinks."

"I'm sorry, Mr. McMahon," I said, "but the five-star hotel up the road was fully booked." I put my bag on the bed nearer the door. "This'll have to do."

"You cannot seriously be suggesting that we're sharing a room?"

"Seriously."

"Oh, this is ridiculous."

I was surprised he was so upset; I thought by now he'd be lying on the bed sucking a lollipop and looking provocatively over the top of his sunglasses. This boy had moods, obviously, and I'd just woken him into a bad one. He went to the little square window at the back of the room and stared out to the rubble-strewn yard beyond.

"What's up?"

No reply.

"Fine." I didn't want to get into it. "I'm going to take a nap."

Nothing.

"That okay with you?"

"Do whatever the fuck you want."

"I will."

"Right."

I lay down on the bed with my hands behind my head. He stood with his back to me, staring out at that dismal view. "Look, kid," I said, "we're going to be on the road together for a few days. I'm sorry about what happened to you, I really am. Your boss obviously thinks this is the best thing to do under the circumstances, and…"

He spun around. "You know nothing about my boss! So shut up!"

"Okay! Okay! I know nothing. Calm down. Jesus."

He turned around again, but not before I'd seen tears come to his eyes. Well, he'd have to deal with that in his own way. If he tried to leave, I'd hear him. But for now I was in no mood to play camp counselor. After a day on the road I needed some shut-eye. Then, maybe, we'd go into town and find somewhere quiet to eat. There was a liquor store half a mile back; we'd get some beers, and watch TV, and the evening would pass somehow. He could tell me about his boss in his own sweet time.

I closed my eyes and relaxed. Gradually the images of endless road faded, and I began to drift off. I heard a creak from nearby, opened my eyes a slit and saw Stirling curled on his bed, his legs drawn up, his back toward me. I don't know if he was still crying.

And I fell asleep.

Sometimes I'm not sure what's a dream and what's a memory. There's a lot of stuff from my military career that I try not to think about—"blocked" is the word that the shrinks would use, but I prefer to say that I don't want to spend my life remembering that shit. It's a choice you make. You see bad things, you don't want to go over and over them in your mind. That's a short cut to the nuthatch. But sometimes it comes back as vivid as a movie whether I want it to or not, when I'm asleep or half awake. I figure out strategy, plan operations, brief my troops and go into action. Sometimes these memories are good. Most times they're bad.

Today they were good—so good they hurt worse than the bad stuff. Fear and injury and death I can deal with—I'm trained for that. But happiness, love—no, they don't train you for that in the USMC. There's no best practice for dealing with love. When I met Will Laurence, I was in unknown territory.

After that first encounter, I noticed him everywhere around the base—walking across the yard, eating his meals, on parade, maintaining vehicles. I was surrounded by fit, young, sexually frustrated marines, and half of them would have been happy to help me out—but they didn't register. Just this one—this slim brown-haired boy from Tennessee or wherever the hell he was from. Okay, I confess, I knew it was Tennessee. I read his file.

When we passed each other he saluted, but he also smiled. No law against that. If I saw him at work and watched him for a while, he always looked up, those grey eyes flashing out at me. He seemed to know when I was there. He seemed to be waiting for me.

And this was the memory that came back to me as I lay on that motel room bed, travel-tired, disorientated, lonely.

The second time we spoke we were both on a weekend furlough. The Fallujah region wasn't exactly bristling with social hotspots, and applications for leave were nonexistent. However, we were required to take a certain amount of R and R, so once every couple of weeks we trundled out in buses to the military base at Lake Habbaniyah, where a makeshift recreation facility had been set up. Some of the old barrack blocks had been turned into canteens, there were volleyball courts and a baseball diamond marked out on compacted earth—and there was the lake to swim in. Beer was doled out in small quantities every evening—never enough to get loaded, of course. The food was a little worse than what we were used to at home base. We were allowed to sleep more—but the sleeping quarters were so fucking hot and airless that it was a pointless indulgence.

I took my furloughs because I had to; I'd rather have worked. But on this occasion I was looking forward to the next 48 hours, because one of the other names on the list was Corporal William Laurence.

I saw him getting on the bus. Nobody grabbed him in one of those complicated handshakes by which the popular guys recognize each other. Nobody play-punched him in the gut or got him in a headlock. He nodded to a couple of people, and they nodded back. He walked past me, smiled and took a seat halfway down the vehicle.

I glanced around. He was dressed in civvies—a faded college T-shirt and a pair of board shorts. Trainers on his feet, no socks.

Nice, I thought, and looked away.

I didn't see him for the next twelve hours. I wouldn't say I was looking for him—that would be too deliberate—let's say instead that I walked around the facility with my eyes open and he was not there. I spent the day reading the newspapers, watching DVDs, doing a bit of paperwork and joining in a game of volleyball when the sun was less fierce. No sign of Will anywhere. Hey ho. Off with his friends.

After dinner I took a stroll around the perimeter; the facility was fenced and heavily guarded, which kind of spoiled the Methodist picnic vibe they were going for. Out by the water's edge there was an old concrete guardhouse that must have been shelled at some point in the last twenty years, and nobody had bothered to pull it down; now, I guess, it was home to a few scorpions and furry critters and not much else. It was known as a place where you could sneak a joint without much danger of being busted; the ground was littered with roaches as well as more conventional cigarette butts. On occasion I'd seen condoms, too, so dope wasn't the only illicit substance being sampled out there. Typical of the USMC to turn a blind eye. As long as nobody officially knew about it, it wasn't a problem.

Tonight there was no smell of dope, no sounds of fucking, just lake waters lapping and the strumming of a guitar. A few soft chords, a bit of picking, the suggestion of a melody.

I walked slowly toward the old guardhouse. The sun was down, and what little light was left in the sky was reflected in the water—and it was against that that I saw the silhouette of a seated figure, head down, back bent, the neck of a guitar sticking out at right angles. I got within ten feet and listened.

I must have shifted, made a noise, because the music stopped.

"Who's there?" The voice was tense and guarded.

"It's okay. Friend."

The figure stood up and faced me. I squinted; there was just enough light to identify the mystery guitarist.

"Corporal Laurence."

"Captain Stagg?" He stood to attention and saluted, swinging the guitar over his back.

"No need for that, Will." I stepped closer. "We're on leave. You can call me Dan." I leaned against the pitted, crumbling concrete wall. "Carry on playing."

"Oh, it's okay. I was only wasting time."

"Nice way to waste it." A roar of voices drifted over the sand. "Better than drinking beer, right?"

"I got beer." He picked up an old canvas rucksack, and there was a chink of glass.

"You came prepared."

"Sure did. Want one?"

"Why not?"

He sat cross-legged on the sandy ground, opened two bottles and handed one to me. I sat too.

"Cheers, Cap'n."

"Cheers, Corp'ral."

We touched the necks of our bottles together and drank, our eyes joined in the gathering darkness, and we both knew at that moment what was going to happen. I reached out—actually watched my hand moving out from my body, as if it was something over which I had no control—and touched the back of his head, feeling the short brown hair, the soft brown skin. Breath whished out of his mouth, and I felt him shudder. I drew him to me, and we kissed.

A soft wind disturbed the surface of the lake and made his guitar strings hum. We carried on kissing. There was another distant roar of male voices, and, from closer at hand, the dry chirp of an insect. Our hands were on each other's shoulders, backs, heads and arms, finding the gap between pants and shirts, traveling up stomachs and chests, mine furry, his smooth. I found his nipples and pinched, and he moaned into my open mouth.

From that point on, the entire senior administration of the USMC could have marched down on us and we wouldn't have been able to stop. I hadn't got laid for weeks, and, by the look of things, neither had Will. He pushed his hands against my chest, broke the kiss and sprang down to the waistband of my shorts, his agile fingers popping the buttons, grabbing the fabric and pulling them down. My ass landed on the sand and gravel, and my dick shot up into the cooling evening air. It didn't get cool for long. Will grabbed it, shuffled back on his knees and opened his mouth. A kiss and a lick were the only preliminaries; his lips engulfed me, slid down the shaft and touched the soft bush of hair. I rested one hand on the back of his head, and with the other caressed his neck, his throat.

The soft breeze was getting harder, sending ripples and then waves to the shoreline, the sound of splashing water mixing with the slurps and clicks of Will's mouth working on my dick. I felt it starting, my thighs tensing, my balls drawing up...

The sound of splashing water. The sensation of a mouth on my cock, my nuts tightening...

I woke up. The shower was running, water splashing loud on cheap white plastic. And there was a mouth on my cock, a head buried in my lap. A blond head, the hair wet. Beads of water on the tanned skin of the back, rolling down the neck.

Stirling McMahon was kneeling at the foot of the bed, his hands on my thighs, his lips working up and down my cock, which he'd pulled through the fly of my shorts.

"Jesus, kid..."

But it was too late to complain. What started in my dream boiled over into reality, flooding his throat with cum. He took it all and swallowed, and did not let me go until I'd pumped out every last drop and was softening in his mouth.

Shit. This wasn't meant to happen.

Why didn't I push him away? Why didn't I tell the

stuck-up little bastard to keep his hands—and mouth—to himself? Why was I stroking his wet hair like this?

Eventually he let me go and crawled up the bed to lie against me. He was naked, his body wet, and I opened my arms and held him. He was hard, of course; I could feel it sticking into my thigh, but he didn't want to do anything, just burrowed against my chest, put one arm across my stomach as if making sure I didn't get away, and we both slept.

An hour later we woke up. The sheets under me were damp, and sweat was pooling where our skin was in contact. "Come on, kid, get up."

"No. Stay here."

"Let's go." I sat up, and he reluctantly rolled away. "Time to eat." I looked at my watch: nine o'clock. I was starving. "There's a diner up the street."

"Okay." He stepped into his shorts—still no underwear—and pulled on a sweatshirt. I might have known: Abercrombie & Fitch. Do they get given an A&F charge card on their eighteenth birthday, these rich kids?

I put on jeans and a sweater, and we walked down the street together. For the first time since I'd met him—since he'd been delivered to me—Stirling seemed happy. He had a spring in his step, he talked like a normal person, and when we got to the restaurant he didn't complain about the menu but ordered a burger and fries and ate the lot. The miserable, sulky little bitch that left New York had been replaced by—well, by a regular guy. Was that all it took—a mouthful of cock, an hour of intimacy and a few gestures of affection? Had his life, his childhood, been so starved of love?

His eyes sparkled as he talked and chewed, and he

laughed like he meant it. And, under the table, his leg kept finding mine.

Shit, I thought. He's falling in love.

**For the next two days we fell into a nice little
routine.** We got up early after sleeping in the same bed,
showered, packed up, got breakfast from the first decent
coffee shop we could find and then drove all day, stopping off for picnics and swims and hikes in the woods.
We talked a lot, but only about immediate things—
nothing about our real lives, our past, let alone our
future. Stirling dropped the fag-brat act, and I treated
him like a human being rather than a parcel to be delivered. Afternoons around five we'd find a quiet motel,
pay up for the night and put our bags into our room. I'd
check in with Ferrari, report our whereabouts and ask
for orders. Nothing—just carry on as instructed. And
then, with the car parked and the curtains drawn, we
took a rest.

After that first time in Richfield Springs, we were
screwing like teenagers. I figured that if I kept Stirling
well-fucked, he'd stay in a good mood. And he wasn't
the only one. You only realize how much you've been
missing sex when you start having it—and now I wanted

it all the time. My judgment flew out the window. Stirling's ass was even better than his mouth, and boy, could he take it. On his back, on his knees, on his side, on top, every which way I could give it. I've had boys that meant more to me than Stirling McMahon—boys that I cared for, and one boy that I loved—but I have never in all my life had a better, more talented fuck. He made Scott from the Downtown Diner look like a fumbling first-timer.

We made our way into the Adirondacks and spent the night in the most old-fashioned hotel I've ever seen—wooden floors; tall, metal bed frames; and a claw-footed enamel bathtub, no shower. The bed creaked like crazy so we moved to the floor, and if it wasn't for the old hooked rug we'd have been full of splinters. There was a bar downstairs where we ate chicken tenders and drank beer; the old girls who ran the place must have heard us, but they didn't blink an eye. Maybe they were deaf. By ten o'clock, we were "tired" enough to turn in again. I fell asleep at first light, and when I woke, four hours later, Stirling was already sucking my dick.

Thursday was a long drive east, taking the ferry across Lake Champlain and into Vermont, where we stayed in a pretty little town that looked like Stepford, all white fences and "adorable" gift shops. Usual routine: checked in at five, called Ferrari, and by ten thirty I was rolling on a condom. Pit stops at gas stations and supermarkets had been supplemented by visits to drugstores. We were going through a pack a day.

Afterward I went out to get food, leaving Stirling alone for half an hour. When I closed the door he was singing Beyoncé songs in the shower. When I got back he was fully dressed, sitting on the edge of the bed, staring at his feet. He glanced up, then down again. I put the food on the dressing table—some fancy deli wraps that I bought from a stoned-looking woman in a kaftan for at least three times their real value—and ruffled his hair. "Hey, boy."

He flicked his head, pushed my hand away.

Okay—something's up—post-fuck blues, maybe. He'll get over it.

"Hungry?"

"No."

I knew he was. He was always starving after sex.

"Beer?"

He shook his head, didn't even reply. I prized the top off a bottle and handed it to him. "I said no!" His cheeks were red, his eyes dark.

"Fuck! What's up?"

"Nothing. Just stop fussing around me."

Fussing? This from a boy who, about forty-five minutes ago, was performing one of the most elaborate feats of oral stimulation ever attempted on a penis? "Okay, Stirling. Whatever. I'm gonna eat." The wrap was disgusting, like biting into a wet washcloth, but it was fuel. He still didn't speak. I finished eating, glugged the beer and lay back on the bed.

"Wanna watch TV?"

"No."

"Okay."

What the fuck was his problem? Was it the fact that our little road romance was coming to an end? One more day and we'd reach our destination, the White Mountains of New Hampshire. For three days we'd been lost, driving where we wanted, sleeping where we wanted, fucking when we wanted, which seemed to be all the time that we weren't driving or sleeping. After tonight we would slip back into someone else's program. He was a rich-kid "secretary" with a price on his head; I was a disgraced ex-marine and unemployed doorman. It did seem pretty hopeless. I was tempted to start sulking myself.

"Stirling."

Nothing.

I went over to him. "Stirling." He turned away. I reached around and grabbed his chin, stroking it with my thumb. I'm surprised I couldn't feel an indentation in the shape of my balls there, due to natural erosion.

He looked up, and tears spilled down his cheeks. I sat on the bed and put an arm around his shoulders. "Oh, baby, what's the matter?" *Baby?* What the fuck? How did this happen?

"I'm sick of this," he said. "Sick of running away. I'm sick of shitty motel rooms and crappy food and... I'm sick...I'm sick of you."

This was not the impression he'd given me earlier on. Something had happened in the thirty minutes I'd been getting alfalfa sprouts and soggy grated carrot. What? A mental breakdown in half an hour? Seemed unlikely. Stirling's good moods usually lasted well after I'd emptied my nuts in his guts.

Analyze the situation, Stagg. Assess, analyze, act.

"Has someone been here?"

"No."

He wouldn't look me in the eye.

"Have you made a phone call?"

"No." He started kissing and sucking on my thumb—obviously to distract me. I moved my hand.

"Stirling, tell me the truth. Have you been using a phone?"

"No. For fuck's sake." He stood up. "You're not my dad."

"Ah, good. You noticed that, did you? I kind of hoped the message got across."

He walked to the door, looked out at the car.

"You'd better tell me what's wrong."

"Nothing. I'm just upset."

"Why?"

"I'm sorry." He turned around. "Okay? I'm hungry. I'll eat."

I gestured toward his wrap, which was leaking into its recycled paper bag. "Help yourself."

He busied himself with food and tried to make conversation about it, about the weather, our journey, anything. I let him talk.

"Stirling."

"What?"

"I'm waiting."

He wiped his mouth on the back of his hand. "You want it *again?*"

"I don't mean that."

He pouted. "Oh. Shame. I do."

"What happened while I was away?"

"I told you, nothing. Jesus. What do you want? Mr. Happy Face all the time?"

"Tell me the truth."

He frowned.

"Or," I said, "just forget it."

He looked really frightened. "No! Don't say that!" He sat at my feet; without thinking, I stroked his hair. At the roots, right by the scalp, there was a fraction of an inch of dark brown. Whatever fancy shit the hairdressers had been putting on him was growing out, just like the stubble that was starting to appear on his chest. He looked up at me. "I hate this whole situation. When you'd gone, I got thinking...I mean, if it wasn't for my boss and his money, you wouldn't give a damn about me."

"Hey, enough of that."

"It's true."

"Without your boss's money, we'd never have met. Anything that's happened since..." What could I say? Were we *in love*? He was, I guess.

"I've been so happy the last couple of days, and it just hit me—you're on the payroll, like all the rest of them."

"If you think he's paying me for this"—I squeezed my crotch—"you're very much mistaken."

He looked down, and licked his lips. "Maybe not that, then. But—this. Our trip. Our little honeymoon. It's all part of his plan."

"What do you mean? He's getting you out of the city because he's worried about your safety."

"Like, he cares all of a sudden."

"He's your employer, isn't he?" Perhaps it was time to start asking the questions I'd been avoiding so far—like who is the "prominent individual" behind this crazy scheme? Who pays ten-thousand bucks and promises another twenty to do a security job that's worth at best two? Who was giving Ferrari his orders? "Your boss, Stirling..."

"He's a jerk."

"He happens to be a very wealthy jerk. Now come here." I pulled him toward me. "Drop your pants." He did as he was told, and his cock sprang out, half-hard already. He sat on my knee, and we started kissing.

"One more night," I said. "Let's make it a good one."

And we did.

It didn't occur to me—then—that there was anything wrong with this picture. It was just a job, and if I'd got a bit more involved with the cargo than I meant to—well, no harm done. I was getting paid to fuck one of the best pieces of ass in the eastern United States, and I could put up with the occasional bad mood. I felt sorry for the kid; his life must have been pretty grim if he fell in love with a guy like me. It's not like we had a future together. I showed him a bit of kindness, gave him my cock, and he was hearing wedding bells.

I still didn't know who was behind Ferrari, who was paying me—and to tell the truth, I didn't care. Sure, it mattered to me when I lay awake at night, staring up at those damn ceiling fans, listening to the late-night drivers hissing up and down the highway—but most of the time I slept, exhausted by driving, fresh air and fucking. It was a long time since I'd enjoyed the warmth of another body beside me. Hell—on the few occasions when I'd actually managed to spend the night with Will, we were always half-afraid of being busted. For the first time in my life I was where no one could get me, no rules could threaten me, with a man in my arms. Thirty-seven years old, and this was my first taste of freedom, in one anonymous motel room after another, as a bodyguard who'd overstepped his job description. I was well aware of how pathetic that seemed. I don't need anyone else to put me down; I can do that really well myself. But here's something new: I didn't give a shit. Yeah, it could all end tomorrow. Yeah, the whole situation was probably criminal. But Stirling...Stirling did things to me... Stirling made me feel...

Love? No—love was buried in a military graveyard down in Knoxville, Tennessee. Love was over for me; I'd known it once, and I'd never know it again. Love died when a sniper's bullet found its target in Helmand, and Will Laurence was taken away from me in a body bag. That was love: nights by the lake, stolen kisses in the shadows, fucking in outbuildings or offices or empty shower blocks, risking everything for each other. Love was Will deciding to put in for a transfer to Afghanistan when I was posted there, following me no matter what the risks. And it was love that made me forget my training, forget the future and everything I'd worked for and tell those granite-faced bastards with medals where their hearts should be that I was cracking up because Will Laurence had been killed, that I was grieving because the man I loved was dead. Love that left me empty and drifting, unable to go to his funeral, unable even to visit the damn grave...

Stirling was a distraction. A job. A very enjoyable job, for sure; when my cock slid into his silky ass I think I'd have handed back Ferrari's ten grand, it felt so good. And maybe, when the bleach grew out and his body hair came back... But by that time, I'd have delivered him safe and sound to whoever wanted him, and I would never see Stirling McMahon again. Save those fantasies for a rainy day, Stagg. Think about that sweet ass and that pretty mouth on your dick when you're alone in a cruddy rented room in Harlem. You'll need those memories when the money runs out.

We crossed into New Hampshire at midday Friday and drove up into the woods. We had time to kill, and the weather was fine, so I thought we'd spend some time in the great outdoors. Stirling slept most of the way, and when I parked he stayed in the car. Well, I didn't get out of town so often that I was going to miss a chance for a walk in the woods. Stirling wouldn't stray, and if any assassins were smart enough to find him out here in the middle of nowhere, they deserved him. I wouldn't go out of hailing distance.

One New England forest is much like another, and by the time I'd scrambled up a few root-entangled pathways and over a bunch of boulders I'd had enough. I found a clear spot that gave me a view of the sky above and our car below, and I could see Stirling sprawled out in the backseat. In a while I'd wake him up by slapping my cock around his face. He'd like that.

I checked my cell phone. Signal strength had been intermittent, but up here it was clear and strong; I might as well call Ferrari while I had the chance. If we carried on driving, we could be in the White Mountains by evening.

There was only one number in my contacts list, and I hit it.

No answer. *The number you have dialed is not available, please try again later.*

Weird; the whole point of having this damn phone

was to report any problems. For all Ferrari knew, Stirling could have been abducted, shot, strangled, whatever. Await instructions, I'd been told. Report whereabouts, report anything suspicious. Well, this seemed suspicious to me, but who the hell was I going to report it to?

I walked back down to the car; Stirling was still there, fast asleep, looking like something dreamed up by an advertising agency with the Gay Sex account. My dick was stirring—*mouth or ass*, it was thinking, and that's pretty much the extent of its ideas. But my brain was ticking over too.

Who are you, Stirling?

What game are we in?

I knew nothing about him—only what Enrico Ferrari had told me. Stirling was 23, a rich man's son, employed as a secretary by a nameless millionaire who had some very bad enemies. Enemies who wanted to kill the people close to him.

Now, for ten-thousand bucks, let alone the next two installments, I was willing to curb my curiosity and accept things at face value, no matter how implausible they seemed. Ferrari hired me because I was a tough guy; he hadn't asked for my analysis of the situation. But that's the trouble with being an officer in the marines: you don't just learn how to kick asses and break necks. You also learn to ask questions, to understand your enemy's motives.

Was Ferrari the enemy, then? Why was I so suspicious? One unanswered call, a few tall tales, and suddenly I was planning strategies.

You're getting involved, Stagg. You're allowing personal feelings to get in the way of the job. You care about this boy—this boy who means nothing to you—and you're jeopardizing the entire operation.

Yeah, well, shit happens. I reached in through the car window and touched the side of Stirling's face. He hadn't shaved for a couple of days; it suited him.

His eyes opened. "Hey. What time is it?"

"About two."

"We moving on?"

"No hurry. Come on, get up. It's a beautiful day. Stretch those long legs of yours."

He opened the door, got out of the car and stretched. "Mmm. I feel great." He looked around. "Where are we?"

"New Hampshire. Pretty, isn't it?"

His face clouded over. "We're nearly there, aren't we?"

"Forget about that. Let me show you something." I took his hand and led him up into the woods. We climbed for five minutes, squeezing through pine branches and tripping over roots, till we came to a huge boulder where the path turned. The trees stopped abruptly, and we could see for miles across a valley. Forty, maybe fifty miles of uninterrupted wilderness.

"Nice," he said, shading his eyes and gazing out into the blue distance. "Did you bring me up here to fuck me?"

I put an arm around his shoulder. "Maybe. In a while." We looked at the view together, as if we could see the future. "When you've answered a few questions."

"Oh." He squinted; those fancy aviator shades were somewhere in the bottom of his bag. "Like a quiz?"

"Kind of. And if you give the right answers, you get a big prize." I squeezed my crotch. That seemed to be all the encouragement he needed.

"Fire away."

"Question one. Who's your boss?"

Stirling scowled. "Next question?"

"Answer in order, please."

"I can't."

"What do you mean?"

"I'm not supposed to talk about...that."

"Why not?"

"Because it's dangerous." He stepped away from me and stared into the distance.

"And I'm not?"

"You're being paid to look after me." Suddenly he flinched, as if a wasp had stung him. "You are, aren't you? I mean you're not..."

"One of the bad guys? No. You're safe with me."

"Don't scare me like that."

"I need to know."

"Why? He's paying you enough."

"He certainly is."

"So why the questions? I thought you were happy to take the money and run."

He had a point. "Because I don't like mysteries." This was bullshit. Whichever way I dressed it up, I was asking because I was interested. And I was interested because, despite all my instincts, despite my enduring love for Will Laurence and even despite the tinted moisturizer and bleached hair, I was starting to care about Stirling McMahon. Whatever he was—secretary, hustler, rich kid—I had feelings for him. Not just the feelings of dick in ass, of muscle and sweat and skin.

Did he know it? Maybe.

"And supposing I won't tell you?"

"I could leave you here."

"Sure. You could." He turned to me, and his eyes were wet. "Go on, then."

"Who are you scared of, Stirling?"

"You don't understand."

"If you told me, maybe I could help you."

He shook his head.

"Okay, let's try a different question. What happened in New York? What am I protecting you from?"

"Someone tried to kill me."

"Go on."

"I was walking down 54th Street, near my apartment. It was late, about four in the morning—I'd been out with some friends. Not many people about. I was a block away from my building when this car came driving slowly by, right alongside me. I couldn't see who was in it—it had blacked-out windows."

"Go on."

"Well, I thought it was just some guy trying to pick me up. You know, it happens."

"I'm sure it does." If I had a fancy car, and I saw that ass swinging down 54th Street, I might be tempted to have a go myself.

"He pulled up right by me, and so I stopped to see what he wanted. The window rolled down and I could see this guy inside. Jesus."

"What?"

"He had a gun in his hand, and he was pointing it straight into my face."

"Did he fire it?"

"Yes. I think so."

"You think so?"

"I kind of freaked out. I screamed and ran, and then I fell over on the sidewalk, and by the time I got up the car had gone."

"You didn't hear a shot?"

"I'm not sure. Silencer, maybe."

"You've been watching too much TV. If someone shoots at you at that range, you know about it."

"I was scared. I wasn't thinking straight."

"So what did you do?"

"I got up to my apartment and I made a phone call."

"The police?"

"No way. My...employer."

"Why him?"

"Because he'd told me something like this might happen. There had been threats."

"Against you, specifically?"

"That's what he told me."

"Why?"

"Because he has enemies."

"So they shoot *him*. They don't shoot his secretary."

"It's a warning."

"You first, then him?"

"Me first, then his wife, then his kids, then him."

"Nice to know where you stand in the pecking order, isn't it?"

Stirling shrugged. "He was going to leave his wife, actually."

"For you?"

"That's what he said—"

He shut his mouth suddenly, realizing he'd given away too much. I wanted to say, "Oh, come on, Stirling, I wasn't born yesterday. Rich old men like your boss only pay beautiful young guys like you for one reason, and it ain't dictation." But I felt sorry for him. Whoever was pulling the strings, Stirling was just as much of a puppet as I was.

"Okay. It's none of my business." I put an arm around his shoulders. We sat quiet for a while, looking out at the view. Miles and miles of nothing. A man could lose himself out there, hide away, and nobody could find him. What was stopping us? A shack in the woods far from prying eyes, no neighbors, no phones, we could live like wild men—I could grow a beard, and Stirling could stop waxing and plucking and bleaching. We could trap our own food, clean it and cook it over a fire, and then I could fuck him under the stars on a mattress of pine needles...

Yeah, and knowing my luck I'd land dick first in a patch of poison ivy. It was a nice little dream, but it was about as realistic as the U.S. Marine Corps handing me the Medal of Honor. I don't know what Stirling was thinking: he had his own dreams, and he wasn't sharing them with me. But we sat together, my arm around his shoulders, his head resting on mine, with nothing to disturb us but the song of the birds, the buzzing of flies and the soft breeze that ruffled his hair. I'm well beyond ruffling.

"Dan." I was half-asleep, and his voice made me start.

"What?"

He rubbed his face against my neck. "You know what I said last night?"

"You said a lot last night."

"About how this was just a job, and you were only being nice to me because you were paid for it?"

"Don't start that again."

"Can I tell you something?"

"Go on." Here it comes: the identity of his boss. The key to the mystery, the explanation of all this "secretary" bullshit. I braced myself. Prominent politician? Church leader? Celebrity?

"I don't really care anymore."

"What do you mean?"

"If they take it all away from me tomorrow—you know, when the job's over—if I have to go back to New York and start all over again." He kissed my neck, just at the point where the stubble turns into chest hair. "Even if they kill me."

"Hey. Don't say that."

"Because if it all has to end..." He kissed me again. "I'm glad we had this. These last few days have been... you know."

"I know." I'm not used to this kind of talk. Even during the best times with Will—a couple of nights we spent in a hotel in Kabul, of all places, away from military jurisdiction—we expressed ourselves through action rather than words. Now I felt awkward, and it was easier for me to kiss Stirling on the mouth than to let him carry on talking.

He kissed me back like he meant it—not the expert kiss of the professional lover, this was urgent, almost desperate, joining our mouths as if he was afraid we'd be torn apart.

"Jesus, kid..."

"Make love to me, Dan. Please."

"Let's get back to the car, at least."

"Now." He extended his legs; his shorts were bulging at the front. Stirling had good legs, long, lean, defined—dancer's legs, you might call them, and he could get them higher and wider than anyone else I knew. I ran a hand from his ankle up his calf to his thigh, feeling the stubble growing back, the muscles taut under the skin. You must remember that we'd only been fucking for a few days under strange and dangerous circumstances; it's a tough combination to resist. And out here in the open air with the smell of the trees and the chirping of the chickadees, it seemed like the most natural thing in the world.

And my dick was ready. Boy, was it ready. It was like an iron bar in my pants, and if I didn't give it some freedom soon it was going to hurt.

My fingers found the button on Stirling's shorts, and with one quick twist it was open. I tugged at the waistband, he shifted his ass on the rock and down they came. Underwear? Come on.

Stirling's cock was as stiff as mine—as stiff as a fuck-hungry 23-year-old's dick can be. It wasn't the biggest in the world—he loved comparing it to mine, pressing our rods together in his hand and saying something like "You're so *big!*" knowing exactly what effect those words have on a man. But it sure was pretty. I'm not a great one for poetry, but sometimes when I looked at Stirling's prick, I thought about roses and ivory and all the usual bullshit. It tasted as good as it looked, and I'd even begun to think—yeah, this is how far gone I was— that I might let him try sticking it up my ass. Romantic fool, right?

He kicked his shorts over his feet, and they disappeared somewhere down the hillside far below us. We didn't care. I just wanted him naked, and the sooner I got him impaled on my cock the better. If anyone in the woods had powerful binoculars they were about to get a world-class sex show. I pulled his T-shirt over his head; all he had left on were his trainers and socks.

I moved myself so I was sitting behind him, legs on either side of his ass, holding him with one arm, pinching his tits and gently stroking his cock. I knew that Stirling liked nothing better than for me to keep fucking him after he'd come; this time, he was going to have to give me one load before I'd even enter him. He seemed to understand. He stretched his arms up and back, clasping his hands at the back of my neck, and closed his eyes. Looking over his shoulder I could see every ridge of muscle, every glisten of sunlight on pale hair, could see the pearl of precum gathering at the tip of his prick. I kissed him, scratching his face with my chin, and he tensed. The first volley shot out into the void, landing with a splat on the leaves below; two, three, four followed it.

I lay him down gently on the rock, inhaling the yeasty smell of his sweat and semen, and fished around in my pants pocket. One thing I'd learned from a few days with Stirling McMahon: never go anywhere without a condom. I unzipped and pulled my dick out. One, two, three downward strokes and it was sheathed with its second skin, the latex crinkling behind the flared head. All that remained was to decide which way I wanted him. One position was all that was needed; this was not going to take long.

I glanced down at his face, and decided: that was what I wanted to see as I fucked him. His back's very nice, the long trapezius muscles leading up from his ass to his shoulders, but right now I wanted to stare into his eyes and kiss him on the lips and see the mixture of pain and pleasure moving across his features. I knelt, grabbed his knees and swiveled him around. Stirling's agile, especially when he knows he's going to get fucked, and he practically jumped into position, pulling his legs back and showing me his pink hole. I spat in my hand, plastered it over my cock and lined up the target.

I slid into him, feeling the smoothness of his ass against my dick, watching his brows contract as he bit his lower lip. His dick was small and soft, shrinking back into his body, the last few drops of semen oozing out into his trimmed bush. With most guys, this would be unfair—they don't like to get fucked unless they're as hard as I was, otherwise it hurts too much. Not so for Stirling. For him, it just heightened the sensation. I let myself rest inside him, feeling my dick swelling to its maximum size, stretching him from inside.

I started to fuck him, slowly at first, all the way out until only the head was engaged, then all the way in.

Remember those old-fashioned balloon pumps that we used to have at kids' birthday parties? You fitted the little limp bit of rubber over the nozzle at the end, then you pumped the big cylindrical cardboard plunger in and out, watching the balloon stand up and swell, growing and growing until one more pump would make it burst. That's the effect my fucking had on Stirling's dick. For the first few strokes, it lay there like a shriveled mushroom. Then it began to stir. It seemed to stretch itself, elongating against his groin, the head aiming for his navel. Each thrust of my dick into his ass pumped more blood into his prick. And when it was halfway there, it launched itself into the air, cantilevering away from the body, getting longer and thicker until the skin, so recently wrinkled, was tight and shiny.

I fucked him harder, holding his ankles in my hands, staring down into his face, knowing that I possessed him as completely as one human being can possess another.

I said it wouldn't take long, and it didn't. I'd just about got up to ramming speed when I felt my nuts tighten, felt my orgasm starting somewhere deep in my belly, traveling upward and outward until there was no stopping it. I leaned forward, cupped his head in my hand and hammered into him, shooting hard and heavy up his ass. With the last thrust I righted myself, just in time to see his hand fly to his cock and milk out another load—less forceful than before, it landed in glistening milky puddles on his tight stomach, pooled for a while then ran down his lean sides.

We didn't say much while we disengaged and started to dress. For once, my head was empty: no worries, no theories, no thoughts.

"Hey, Dan." He was pointing over the edge, beyond the boulder. Way down where it would take ropes and pulleys to reach them was a pair of denim cut-offs. I slapped his ass and shoved my boxers in his face. We wrestled a bit, and eventually he put them on. I pulled my jeans over my bare ass and laced up my shoes.

Not a moment too soon. There were voices through the trees, figures climbing up the slope toward us. Two men, blue shirts, dark blue pants.

Cops.

I hadn't heard a car, but that's not surprising; they could have landed a helicopter and I wouldn't have noticed, not while I was fucking that ass.

Operational misjudgment, Stagg. Bad mistake. What had they seen? The last thing we needed was to be busted for lewd behavior, indecent exposure or whatever charge they bring for open-air fucking in New Hampshire.

"Hey, officers." It's always best to initiate conversation with potential hostiles. Start off friendly, things might just not be so bad.

They looked us up and down; it didn't take Sherlock Holmes to figure out what we'd been doing. Stirling's slim belly, visible through his unbuttoned shirt, was glistening with jizz.

"Is that your car parked below, sir?"

"Sir" rather than "faggot" or "asshole"—always a good sign, I think.

"Yup. Rental."

"Can you tell us the license number?"

"Sure." I had the keys in my pocket, and the number was on the fob.

"And the point of origin?"

"I guess you know that already, officer." Start off friendly, I said—but establish boundaries. If the cops had something to say, let 'em say it.

"What's your name?"

"I beg your pardon, sergeant?" I know how to speak to inferiors, and he recognized the tone.

"Sir. What's your name, sir?"

"Stagg. Dan Stagg." I almost added "Major," but they took that title from me along with everything else.

The two cops looked at each other; one of them shook his head. Then they both looked at Stirling. "And you, sir?"

Without missing a beat, he said "Jody Miller."

"Miller?"

"Yes, sir," said Stirling. "Jody Miller. M-i-l-l—"

"Miller. Sure. I got it," said the cop. They looked at each other again, shifting from foot to foot like they were standing in an ants' nest.

"Is there a problem?" I asked, folding my arms across my chest. Old security guard's trick. Let the customer see your muscles. It kind of calms them down. Okay, these were New Hampshire state cops, but the same principle applies.

"No problem, sir. We're looking for a missing person."

"Uh-huh."

"A young man…well, about your age, Mr. Miller."

"Uh-huh." Ask no questions, and you won't get any smart answers.

Silence for a moment, apart from the usual buzzing and squawking.

"Well, you have a nice day now," said the sergeant. "Drive carefully."

We followed them back down the track, got into the car and drove off at a slow and sensible speed. It was only when they were well out of view, and there was no sign of pursuit in the rearview mirror, that I breathed a sigh of relief and said, "Jody Miller? Where the hell did that come from?"

Stirling was silent for a while, looking out the window. Then he turned to me and said, "That's my name."

"I'm waiting."

We were sitting in a bar in Lincoln, New Hampshire. The town was dead—only one motel was open, the Starlight on Main Street, so we checked in and went in search of beer and food. We found a folksy diner; in ski season they'd be five deep at the bar, but now we were the only people in the place. That suited me fine.

Stirling—Jody—whatever his name was—stared out the window. Cars and trucks went up and down the road. There wasn't much to look at.

"Come on."

"Jody Miller. That's me." He wiped wet eyes with the back of his hand and straightened his shoulders. Good start, I thought. I'll make a man of you yet. "Or Muller, if you want to be picky. My grandfather was German."

"Okay."

"Changed it to Miller when they came over after the War. That's what my Mom told me, anyway."

"So, Jody Miller." I stuck my hand out. He shook it, held it for a moment. "Pleased to meet you. And what's with the fancy alias?"

"Jody Miller was a sad little boy from a shitty town in Michigan who went to a correctional facility at the age of fourteen. I didn't want to be him anymore."

"Fair enough. Why'd they lock you up?"

He put his fingers through his hair; I swear those dark roots were getting longer. "Hustling."

"At fourteen?" I whistled. "Boy, you were an early starter."

"You can thank one of my mom's boyfriends for that. Oh, and there was stealing as well. Theft to order, the judge called it."

"Nice."

"When I got out I was nearly seventeen, and I thought, well, I can hang around in Michigan for the rest of my life, servicing dirty old men till I get some fatal disease or one of them murders me, or I can get my ass to New York City and make a new start."

"What did your parents say to that?"

He laughed—the kind of laugh that's far worse than crying. "My dad disappeared when I was born. My mom...she had a few problems with drugs."

"Shit."

"Yeah, well." He fiddled with his nails, the kind of gesture that usually drives me crazy, but under the circumstances I could put up with it. "Made me grow up quick, I guess. I could take care of myself. I've got that to thank her for."

"And is she...?"

"Dead?" His voice was flat as he watched a huge

load of logs laboring up the road. "I don't know. Don't really care."

Now was not the time to tell him to be a dutiful son and respect his mother. I'm no great example of family life myself. "So you ran away."

"If you can call it that. I don't think she noticed. Nobody came looking for me."

"To New York?"

"I wanted to be an actor. Yeah, you can laugh, but I was cute back then."

"You're cute now."

"Maybe." He ran his fingers through his hair. "Takes a lot more work these days. When you're seventeen you don't have to try."

"What happened?"

"I got a few breaks. A pretty face will get you that far. Did a couple of acting jobs, bit of modeling... But there were easier ways of making money." He sighed again. "Anyway, I didn't have any talent. Not for acting, anyway." He looked at his dirty fingernails. "Fuck. I'm falling to pieces."

"So you went back to hustling."

"Very clever, Major Stagg. Only you don't call it that anymore. You get a profile on a fancy website, and you call yourself a masseur or a personal trainer. That way you get the rich clients."

"Like your boss?"

He hesitated, reached a decision and said, "Like my boss. Julian Marshall the Second."

The name rang a bell from the New York papers. "Businessman?"

"Property developer. Marshall Land."

"Big man."

"Yeah." Stirling—I mean Jody—allowed himself a smile. "Big and fat."

"And rich."

"And old and ugly. But he was nice to me. At first."

His voice sounded shaky again, and I went to the bar to order some food. When I got back to the table he had the beer bottle in his hand, and looked calmer.

"Let's drink to something," he said.

"What did you have in mind?"

"How about honesty?"

"Honesty." We tapped our bottles together, each drank half. "So tell me about Julian Marshall the Second."

"It started four years ago. Let me think—yeah, it was spring, I was wearing this new shirt I got in the Armani sale. It was gorgeous."

"Not interested."

"Sorry, but sometimes the only way I can remember things is by what I'm wearing. Anyway, it was spring four years ago, and I got an email from a guy who wanted a companion for a weekend trip."

"Sounds nice."

"That's the kind of stuff I did. Better than going to a hotel room for an hour. Pays well, you get to see nice places and eat in nice restaurants and—well, you get to share a bed for the night. I charge more for it, but I like it. It's comforting, even with a man like him."

"Go on."

"I was living with three other actors in Brooklyn, in a really small sublet apartment that was only meant for two. It was, you know—grungy. And this guy sent his chauffeur to collect me in a limo. Can you imagine? A big, shiny black car pulling up outside our building. My roommates were all hanging out the window as I walked out in my Armani shirt, with a weekend bag, it was Chanel that bag, or at least it was supposed to be."

"Try to remember that I don't care about labels."

"We drove to the Upper West Side and waited outside. The driver was this Italian guy, really handsome, and I tried to make conversation with him, but he wasn't the talkative type."

"Ferrari?"

"Yeah, Ferrari." Jody sighed. "I never did get to suck his cock. Anyway, after half an hour the old guy came out, big and fat, in the worst kind of resort wear you could imagine, and I'm like—Jesus, if you're that rich can't you afford some decent clothes?"

"And that was Marshall?"

"Yes. Although he told me his name was Smith. Can you believe it? I've had so many Mr. Smiths the whole family must be queer."

"What was the deal?"

"I was to be his secretary for the weekend. He was going down to his place in Connecticut to prepare a speech and he needed someone to take dictation. Oh, please! Dictation." He laughed. "But you have to play along with this shit, so while we were driving out of town I told him that I could do shorthand and typing and yes, I'd be happy to help him with his frozen shoulder, I was a fully qualified sports masseur, blah, blah, blah. He kept touching my arm, my leg—not groping or anything, just little dabs. He had really soft hands—kind of fat, with manicured nails. That's such a giveaway. He pretended to be the big family man but one look at those nails and I knew his game."

"And what was that?"

"Nothing fancy. Father-son stuff. Bit of spanking. Getting me to walk around in a pair of gym shorts and tube socks, telling me how disgusting I was, putting me over his knee. He couldn't really get it up."

"Easy money, then."

"He liked the sound of his own voice—lecturing me while I was showing off for him, telling me I was going to hell. He was big on the religion. That was kind of funny."

"And after that first weekend?"

"He hired me again. Repeat business—that's what you're always looking for. I knew just what he wanted, and I was a good enough actor to pretend that I was there to help him with his work. We'd get talking about my sinful lifestyle and the more I confessed, the more he liked it. If I said I was truly repentant he'd spank me and let me jerk off. One day I had a brainstorm, and I burst into tears while I was telling him some stupid sob story, and he nearly had a heart attack. He had his hand down his pants, and I think he might actually have shot his wad that time."

"Jesus."

"Pathetic, isn't it? But he was paying me a thousand bucks for a weekend. That's a lot of money."

"You obviously gave satisfaction."

"You can sneer all you like, Dan, but it's better than killing people for a living."

"You're probably right."

"Anyway, it got to the point where he offered to

set me up in an apartment with a regular allowance. He'd see me when he was in town, or we'd go down to Connecticut for weekends. He even took me with him to conferences, and I was always introduced as his secretary. I don't think anyone was fooled, but believe me I wasn't the only one. A lot of those business leaders have personal assistants or drivers or translators, men or women. We didn't talk to each other, that was one of the rules, and if you were introduced you just kept your mouth shut. But we all knew. Jesus, some of the guys I recognized from the clubs and gyms. Nobody was fooled. All these fat old men and their pretty young companions. All of them big believers in family values."

"Did his wife know?"

"She doesn't care. Nobody wanted to rock the boat, and Marshall trusted me to keep my mouth shut. After a couple of years I was his exclusive property. He owned the place where I lived, he was my only source of income, and he didn't like me going with anyone else. I took my profiles down, and if I tried to meet other guys he always knew about it. I felt like I was being followed every time I left the house."

"And were you?"

"They told me that if I ever opened my mouth I would disappear, just like that. I knew too much."

"You knew Marshall was gay."

"More than that."

"Criminal stuff?"

He nodded, and just then the food arrived. The waitress fussed around with mustard and mayo and eventually left us alone. We waited till she was well out of earshot, and Jody continued.

"Once in a while, Marshall used me for other jobs. 'Entertaining' his business associates. If they wanted a girl, Ferrari found them a girl. If they wanted a boy, he sent me."

"Thought you said he was jealous?"

"Not if I was useful to him. Sometimes I just had to take these old guys out for dinner, sometimes they wanted sex. Some of them weren't too bad. Better than Marshall. But afterward, he wanted all the details, everything they'd said and done."

"Blackmail?"

"At first I thought he was just a dirty old man. But eventually I realized there was more to it than that. He was using me—and Ferrari made all the arrangements."

"What kind of arrangements?"

"Dinner dates. Weekend trips. They were always rich-looking older guys. Some of them liked to talk, so I knew what they were—politicians, property inspectors, that sort of thing."

I could hear them now, the fat cats talking themselves up to impress the cute kid with the available ass. "So Marshall used you to sweeten his deals?"

"I guess." He frowned.

"And if they wouldn't play ball, he threatened them with exposure?"

Jody drew pictures with his finger on the table top. Marshall's business style was becoming a lot clearer to me—he bribed the right people with sex and money, but if they refused to support his crooked property deals he turned to blackmail. A profitable sideline for Julian Marshall, or his core business? Was this why he wanted

Jody out of town in such a hurry? Was he covering his tracks? I never bought that story about the gunman in 54th Street. Who tries to kill a secretary—or even a hustler? But if Marshall was under investigation...

I met Jody's troubled gaze. He wanted to tell the truth; my dick had got me that far.

A couple of locals walked into the bar and sat down nearby, eyeing us with hostile suspicion. "Come on," I said, "let's eat up and leave." I paid, and we walked slowly back toward the motel. "Nobody can hear us on the street."

He didn't talk for a while, just fell into step with me and, every so often when there were no vehicles near us, reached for my hand. We overshot the motel and headed out of town, where the sidewalk ran out and there was nothing but grass and trees and a rapidly dwindling twilight.

"It all changed when Peters died."

"Who was Peters?"

"Trey Peters. Sounds like a movie star, right? Looked like a bum. Sleazy bastard, never as clean as he should have been. I hated going with him."

It wasn't just the cool evening air that made me shudder.

"He worked for Marshall a long time back, then left to set up his own company. Started off as a property inspector, then he became a developer in his own right. Not as big as Marshall Land, but big enough to be a rival."

"And I thought you were too dumb to understand what was going on."

"I went with Peters a couple of times to hotel rooms,

didn't think much about it. Then one day, Ferrari told me to go in with a wire."

"Did he say why?"

"He told me that Peters was back in the firm now, that he and Marshall had cut a sweet deal over a development in Queens and that to celebrate I was going to look after Mr. Peters and do anything he wanted to do."

"So they sent you in with recording equipment."

"Just a tiny little thing, no bigger than a quarter, sewn into my jacket pocket. I didn't even have to switch it on."

"Sounds like Mr. Marshall has a fancy surveillance operation."

"My only instructions were to do whatever Mr. Peters wanted, and if I took my jacket off—if!—to leave it no more than four feet away. He was staying in a hotel on the Upper West Side; the suite was bigger than the house I grew up in. Huge bathroom, whirlpool, room service, the works. All of it paid for by Marshall Land."

"A trap."

"It was so easy. Peters started talking dirty the minute I walked in the door, getting me to strip for him, telling me everything he wanted to do to me. I gave him the full show, throwing my clothes around the room— making sure that the jacket landed in the right place, of course. After a while he wanted to move into the bathroom, so I had to think fast. I told him I had something special for him in my jacket pocket—a couple of tabs of Viagra. Oh, yeah! He was like a kid in a candy store! I hung my jacket over the back of the bathroom door and just hoped that the sound of the whirlpool wouldn't be too loud."

"Very conscientious of you."

"I'm a professional," said Jody, grabbing my hand and bringing it to his ass. "At least, I was. So we took our pills and we fucked all over the bathroom, and at least I had a chance to clean him up a bit. Peters was one of those guys who likes to tell you what they're doing to you while they're doing it—even if they can't do it properly—so he gave Marshall and Ferrari everything they needed. We finished off in the bedroom, and he got very grouchy with me. Called me a lot of nasty names. They're like that, the Trey Peterses of this world. One minute they love you, the next minute they hate you. And I thought well, asshole, you'll get what's coming. I got dressed and said goodbye and that was that. Job done. A week later, it was on the news."

"He was dead."

"Right. Car accident. He'd gone straight into one of the pillars under a railway bridge in Queens. Police were looking for witnesses."

"I take it you didn't go forward."

"I didn't see anything."

"Of course not. And you didn't say anything to Marshall."

"No."

"How long ago was this?"

"Four or five months."

"Okay." It was dark now, away from the street-lights of Lincoln, and I put my arms around Jody and kissed him on the mouth. I hated what had happened to him—neglected by his junkie mother, abused by her boyfriends, busted, imprisoned, fucked by fat old men who despised him—and I wanted to make it all better.

And how the hell are you going to do that, Dan? Stick another dick in his ass?

"Come on," I said after a while, "it's getting cold. Let's go back to the motel."

We retraced our steps. "I didn't hear from Mr. Marshall for a few weeks after that, and I started to get worried. The rent was still paid on the apartment, and Ferrari would deliver money, but Marshall himself never wanted to see me and never even called. I knew he had to be careful with his wife and his business associates, and he always told me to be patient, that one day we'd be together properly. But after a while I just couldn't stand it anymore, and I went to his office."

"I bet he was pleased to see you."

Jody ignored the sarcasm. "Yes, he was actually. He'd just been really busy with this deal that was going through, and his wife was being very demanding. He apologized."

"Great."

"And he was worried about the Trey Peters business."

"I bet he was." Who was on Marshall's back, I wondered: the police? The District Attorney?

"He asked if anyone had tried to talk to me about Mr. Peters, and I said of course not, and even if they did I would never say a word."

"That must have been a relief to him."

"And that's when he suggested I should maybe get out of town for a while, until it had all blown over."

"I see. And was this before or after someone tried to shoot you in 54th Street?"

"Oh." We were close to the motel now, and he looked as if he wanted to run. "I...I can't remember."

"Because that sort of thing is easy to forget, right?"

We walked into the darkness between streetlights. Jody stood close enough to whisper. "That never happened."

"No shit."

"It's what they told me to tell you, if you asked any questions."

"They must think I'm dumb."

Jody shrugged. "I was never a very good actor. I'm sorry."

"And why are you telling me the truth now?" If this is the truth, I thought.

"Because...you know. Us."

"Right." I could feel the heat from his body. The motel room was twenty paces away and in it, a bed. My cock stiffened. Down, boy. Talk first, fuck later. "So the real reason Marshall wanted you out of town was to avoid any awkward questions about Trey Peters?"

"Yeah."

"And you went along like a good little boy?"

"No. I thought he was trying to get rid of me, because he was tired of me. So I told him that if I did this for him, he'd have to do something for me."

"And what was that?"

"Leave his wife."

I whistled. "You drive a hard bargain."

"You can laugh, Dan, but Marshall's all I've got. If I lose him, I'm back on the streets."

"Okay. I'm sorry. What did he say?"

"He promised that as soon as things were back to normal he was going to tell his wife about us, and we were going to live together. He's got a place down in

Connecticut, right on the coast. He showed me pictures." Jody sighed. "It looked so nice."

"Who was Marshall frightened of? The police? Were they the ones who were asking questions?"

"He didn't say. Just that people might want to talk to me, and if they knew that I'd been intimate with Mr. Peters they might jump to conclusions."

"Yeah," I said. "The right conclusions. Don't you realize that you're an accessory to murder?"

Jody frowned; the word "accessory" meant something different to him. I was about to explain, when a car door slammed a few feet away from us; Jody jumped like a rabbit.

It was nothing, just an old couple turning up at the motel for the evening, hauling their ugly floral luggage out of their trunk. We laughed at ourselves for being so damn nervous.

"Come on, kid," I said. "We'll talk about this in the morning. And in the meantime, let's see what kind of trouble we can get up to in Lincoln, New Hampshire."

The old couple checked into the room next door. I hoped for their sake they were hard of hearing, because there was going to be a lot of thumping and yelling before any of us got any sleep.

Before the fun began, I called Ferrari. After the missed call in the afternoon I'd been entertaining all sorts of crazy suspicions—Ferrari was playing his own game, using us as pawns in some attempt to work a number on Marshall—and I half expected the line to be dead now. But no—he picked up on the second ring, as cool and calm as ever.

"Ferrari, it's Stagg."

"Good. Where are you?"

"Lincoln, New Hampshire. The Starlight Motel."

"Fine, fine." He paused for a moment, took a breath as if he was about to ask a question, then thought better of it.

"Where were you when I called earlier, Ferrari?"

"On the subway."

I didn't question it; hey, people in New York City *do* use the subway. "Everything okay at your end?"

"Yeah. How's Stirling?" Was there the slightest undue emphasis on the name—as if he was testing me?

"Stirling's behaving himself."

"Good." Another pause. "Stay where you are and await further instructions."

"What about my money?"

"That will be delivered to you."

"It better be."

"I'll call you." He seemed in a hurry and terminated the call. Asshole, I thought, slinging the phone down on the bedside table, and then Jody came out of the bathroom wearing just white sports socks and trainers, and I kind of got distracted.

Dick, ass, this way up, that way up, shower, bed, sleep. Repeat with variations as required. It was better than ever because I cared about him, because he had told me the truth, and that's all I'm going to say on that score.

I woke up suddenly. What woke me? Nothing moving, just the rise and fall of Jody's chest. It was dark in the room, but not so dark that I couldn't scan—from the bathroom to the forecourt, nothing out of place, nothing unexpected. Relax, Stagg, you've got the jitters. It's that business with Ferrari, the unanswered call, everything that Jody told you—go back to sleep, tomorrow is another day. Before closing my eyes I picked up my phone to check the time. The screen lit up: 4:15.

Then I heard it—the faintest click-click, could have been an insect, could have been something in my own ear, but it wasn't. Click-click. It was coming from the door. A key in the lock? Analyze, assess, act. My gun was on the dressing table. I could jump over Jody and be armed and on my feet within five...

The door swung open with a creak that would have woken any civilian. Jody stirred and murmured, "Wha...?," but I hushed him with a hand. A man stepped into the room, silhouetted against the streetlights. It didn't take much to figure out that he was armed. I was naked and defenseless. Wait a minute. A marine is never defenseless. I had the cell phone Ferrari had given me—a block of metal, glass and rigid plastic, maybe six inches by three inches. Properly used, it could kill.

If this had been a simple hit he'd have shot us from the door and made a getaway. Not much you can do about that, just hope he's a lousy marksman—and who hires a lousy marksman for an assassination job? But that wasn't the deal. Any rookie can tell the difference between a shot fired from eight feet away, and a shot fired at close quarters. This was meant to look like a nice cozy domestic killing. No third parties involved.

He crept toward the bed, unaware that we'd woken. I lay still, and thank god Jody got the message—we're in trouble, don't move a muscle. One step closer. Another step. Another. Close enough to hear him breathing. Close enough to smell the cigarette he'd been smoking a few moments ago. Nervous, asshole? Don't you know cigarettes are bad for your health?

He extended his hand. The gun gleamed in the dim light. The safety must have been off already—maybe that's what woke me up. Click-click. Nearer it came, nearer my head, but it was not yet near enough. He wanted point blank.

I shot my arm out from my side, grabbing his wrist with pinpoint accuracy. His reflexes were quick—he pulled the trigger before I disabled him—but not quick enough. The bullet skimmed the surface of the blanket and hit the dressing table mirror with a crash. I sprang to my feet, twisted the man's arm hard and fast enough to dislocate his shoulder, then brought the short end of the cell phone smashing down into his temple. He hardly made a sound, just a gasp as the ball popped out of the socket and a faint "Oof" as the breath left his body. I had no time to see if he was dead or alive.

Jody was up, jumping from foot to foot—he was starting to panic, and if I didn't stop him he was going to blunder into the shards of broken mirror on the floor. I reckoned we had about thirty seconds to get into the car before someone came calling—that shot was loud, and I didn't feel like answering questions. Particularly if the guy on the floor was dead.

I grabbed Jody by the shoulders; the light from the open door showed the shock on his face. "Listen to me, Jody. Put some pants and shoes on, then sit on the bed." He did as he was told, not saying a word. I threw a few things into my bag—gun, cell phone, clothes. The money was safe. "Come on." I pushed Jody through the door and on to the forecourt.

And before we checked out, on a sudden impulse, I took the gun from the assassin's hand, put the safety on and checked it over. Like I said, I'm no great weapons expert—I can't tell you the make and model at a glance, but I just don't believe in wasting perfectly serviceable firearms, even if they have just been leveled at my temple.

But it only took a single glance to see that this wasn't any old gun. This was a Glock 19.

Just the same as mine.

The Cabin 6

The priority was to get as far away from Lincoln as we could, then ditch the car. Every cop in the state would have our license plate within the hour.

But why run? Why not wait on the motel forecourt for the police to rescue us? Why not call them ourselves? We'd just been attacked in our bed by an armed intruder, and if I'd fought him off—if I'd killed him—it was self-defense. An American's home, even if it's just rented for the night, is sacrosanct. He was the bad guy, not me.

But there was something about the whole setup that was making this American very suspicious. The police that stopped us back up the road, looking for someone "about your age"—who the hell were they reporting to, and why were they looking for us? The missed phone call, and Ferrari's evasive, nervous manner when we spoke—just stay where you are, Dan. Wait for further instructions. Yeah—like a bullet in the brain. That certainly tells you where you stand.

And to cap it all—the one thing that really made me suspicious—that old couple that booked into the next-door room. You probably think I'm crazy, that I'm about to hole up in the woods and form a private militia, but that was the final detail that convinced me we'd been set up. Two convenient credible witnesses just the other side of the wall. Not in the room down at the end of the block, where they'd have spent an undisturbed night. Slap bang next door. "Yeah, we heard them fighting, we were too scared to go around and intervene, the guy looked dangerous, and then at 4:15 we heard two shots." Police find our bodies in room three at the Starlight Motel. Murder-suicide. Signs of recent sexual activity. A dangerous ex-marine, sacked from his security job for beating up an innocent young man, on the run with a known prostitute—oh, yes, it all made perfect sense. Nothing to connect me to Ferrari or Marshall. Jody Miller—or Stirling McMahon, the witness of Marshall's unpleasant business practices—silenced forever, slain by a psychopath. I hadn't been hired as a bodyguard. I'd been hired as a murder suspect. Sentence passed post-humously. A gun that matched the ballistics report, my prints all over it. History of violence. Perfect.

Try telling that to the police.

But what the hell—we were still innocent. We'd done nothing wrong. If my assailant was dead, whose fault was that?

Do the right thing, Dan, and face the consequences. Turn yourselves in—you're important witnesses, Jody can bring down Marshall and his cronies, the people who would have killed you if your reflexes had been a fraction of a second slower. That was the game-changer. When I left New York City I was just a hired man, happy to take the money without questioning motives. Now someone had tried to kill me—and I had no doubt who was behind the assassin. Julian Marshall had set the whole job up to silence Jody, getting him out of town—out of New York State—with a plausible promise of love and money. Jody, greedy and gullible as he was, went along with it, a lamb to the slaughter. Well, he'd just had a rude awakening, that's for sure.

But what was Marshall's real game? I needed to think things through. If we were going to hand ourselves in, we had to be sure we were safe. If there was anything that Jody wasn't telling me, now was the time to find out.

He barely spoke a word as we drove out of Lincoln. That suited me; I was busy checking my rearview for signs of pursuit, sifting the data whirling through my head. The adrenaline was leveling off a little, my rational mind getting back in control, and I was able to plan.

Get out of Lincoln.

Get rid of the car.

Hide.

We were heading south around the base of the first big mountain, taking a quiet access road. Nobody was following us, although our headlights would be easy to spot if you knew what to look for. At the end of the road, where the blacktop turned into dirt, was the entrance to a big old wrecker's yard. Piled up, parked at crazy angles, wheels removed, jacked up on bricks, rusting and smashed and covered in weeds, were maybe two hundred old cars.

Where better to hide a hot rental vehicle? The place looked abandoned. It could be days—weeks even— before anyone noticed the shiny Chevrolet behind the rusted hulks. And by then Jody and I would be far away. Out of Marshall's reach. Somewhere he hasn't paid the cops. Somewhere they'll listen to the truth.

I drove across the yard, negotiating potholes, and tucked the car between a high-sided Ford van and a pile of stripped chassis. No sign of a night watchman; what was there to guard? Anything of value had been removed years ago. As a final precaution I threw a half-rotted tarpaulin over the roof of the Chevy—just in case they got the helicopters out.

All was quiet as we started to climb the mountain. It was hard work, and dark. We both fell a couple of times. When I judged we'd gone far enough, we stopped to rest. Jody was shivering. Shock was setting in. He was silent, his face pale in the moonlight, eyes unfocused. I needed to find shelter, or I was going to be in trouble. More trouble, that is.

I warmed him as best I could, speaking words of encouragement, and he responded like a robot. Before long I was getting cold, too—no point in both of us going into shutdown. It's not difficult to die in the woods. Back at the trailhead I'd seen some friendly warning signs posted by the Forest Service.

ATTENTION
Try this trail only in you are in top physical condition,
well clothed and carrying extra clothing and food.
Many have died above timberline from exposure.
Turn back at the first sign of bad weather.

We were both in top physical condition—I'd given Jody several thorough examinations—but we didn't have a cracker between us, no water, and hardly any clothes apart from what we were wearing. I had a brace of firearms in case some local bear decided to get in on the act. I wasn't planning on crossing the timberline— the trees gave us cover, and if necessary we could get to the Canadian border on foot in a few days. But right now, with first light in the sky and one very fucked- up young man on my hands, I urgently needed shelter. Food? Roots and berries? Roasted squirrel? Yes, if it came to it. I've done the survival stuff.

We walked on. The trail was easier as daylight penetrated the trees. There wasn't much chance of meeting anyone up here—maybe the more adventurous tourists would go hiking later in the day, but by that time I intended to be well out of their range. All that really worried me were police dogs. We hadn't left too many tracks behind us, but you can't run from a well-trained nose. Two men who haven't had a shower since fucking, both of them sweating, leave quite a trail behind them.

I heard a thud—Jody had walked straight into a tree, forehead first. It would have been funny if we'd just been out hiking, but now it worried me. He seemed confused, and he didn't feel any pain from the graze. A trickle of blood ran into his eyebrow; he didn't even wipe it away.

He was shutting down, near exhaustion.

I took off my shirt and pulled it over his head, dressing him as you'd dress a child, his arms weak and floppy. I held him, trying to warm him, but he was like a rag doll. "Jody! Come on, man. Look at me! It's Dan! Come on, Jody, please!"

Nothing, just unfocused eyes and an open mouth.

I could make some kind of shelter—there was the forest floor covered in pine needles, enough fallen branches to construct a cover, and we'd lie together until he slept and hope for the best. I'd find food and water. We'd make it. Wouldn't we?

A couple of weeks ago, I'd have sat down and despaired. Who cares if I live or die? The sooner I'm off the face of this godforsaken earth the better. Forget it all, the grief and disappointment, and join Will. Not that I believe in the afterlife or anything like that, but at least we'd have something in common. We'd both be dead.

Now, in the White Mountains with corrupt cops at our heels, with a freaked-out hustler who may quite possibly have been telling me a pack of lies for the last few days, I wanted to live. Now that the odds were really against me, all that was left was my training. And what's the prime objective? Survive.

Thanks, Uncle Sam. You took everything I had to give, you chewed me up and spat me out and now here I am with a man in my arms, and I am damn well going to protect him and serve him. We'll make it to a place of safety and we will get justice. Bring on the New Hampshire police, bring on the helicopters, the dogs, the fucking grizzly bears, I'll take 'em all, and I will fucking win.

I propped Jody against a tree, wiped his forehead with a tissue and went to look for wood. Build a shelter, get him in it. Survive.

And there, not more than twelve feet away, was a

cabin. Shielded from the track by a big granite outcrop, shaggy with moss and ferns, a perfect little house made of logs, neatly overlapped at the ends, shutters over the windows, enough crawlspace underneath to keep the whole thing dry. The roof looked sound. In a couple of months when the hunting season got underway we'd have company. Now it was empty.

The padlock was strong but the fixings were as soft as butter. A screwdriver would have made a more elegant job, but my bare hands did the trick.

I couldn't see much inside—after the deceptive twilight of the mountain morning, the interior was just different degrees of dark. But it smelled dry and piney, and it was warmer than outdoors. It would do very nicely.

I hoisted Jody in a fireman's lift and carried him into the cabin like a bridegroom carrying his new wife over the threshold, placed him softly on the floor and tried to look around. Gradually my pupils adjusted, and I saw all I needed to see—a neat, clean cabin, a narrow cot against the wall with blankets and a crocheted cover, shelves and cupboards stocked with provisions, and camping gear. A camp stove, a lamp. Bottled water.

I lay Jody on the bed and unlaced his shoes. By now, safe indoors, I was almost as tired as he was. All I could think of was getting horizontal and closing my eyes. I climbed in beside him, pulled the blankets up to my chin and held him in my arms. We fell asleep.

I had confused fairy-tale dreams: huntsmen finding enchanted princesses in the woods; Goldilocks—with her dark roots showing—stumbling into the home of the three bears; Snow White; Hansel and Gretel lost in the wood; wicked witches and evil queens...

I woke with a start, replaying the events of the night before—the soft click of the safety catch, the door opening silently, the figure framed against the street-lights... Damn, that dream was real.

Mother of god, it was happening again. A figure framed in the doorway just feet from the bed. This time I had my gun by my side.

"Don't move," I said, "or I'll blow your fucking head off." I didn't shout, just a low conversational tone. In the confines of the cabin it sounded loud enough.

"Jesus Christ! Put the fucking gun down, man!" He sounded young, and very frightened. "I'm not going to hurt you!"

Too damn right he wasn't going to hurt us. I jumped out of bed and walked toward him. He backed out of the cabin and I followed, softly closing the door. Jody was sleeping peacefully—no point in waking him for a little disturbance like this. It was bright outside—the sun was past the zenith, so it must have been midafternoon.

"Put your hands behind your head."

He did as he was told, and I had time to take stock. Short, young—maybe twenty, even nineteen—dark hair under a backward baseball cap, greasy blue coveralls open to the waist, nothing underneath. Crooked teeth. Ridiculously long brown eyelashes. A hairy chest.

I frisked him. He had a screwdriver in one pocket, a spanner in the other. Dangerous weapons in the right hands, but I guess he only used them to fix up cars. What we had here was a real live grease monkey, captured in the wild. I took the tools, and while I was searching his legs for blades or hammers I had an eye-level view of a thickly-furred stomach disappearing into the warm darkness of his dungarees.

"Who the fuck are you?"

I stood up; I was a good six, seven inches taller than him, and even though I was only wearing a tank top and shorts, my feet bare on the forest floor, I had every advantage. He looked scared, and with good reason.

"My name's Kenny," he stammered, looking as if he might bolt for the trees at any second. "That's my dad's cabin."

"Oh, is it?" I scratched my chin and took a good look at him. He was cute in a fuzzy, grungy kind of way. Reminded me of the raw recruits I'd known in my service days. Natural-born respecters of authority, not too smart, easy to discipline. In the wrong hands, easy to brainwash. "Well, now, Kenny, you don't have to go running back to town to tell your daddy that he's got guests, do you?"

"No, sir."

Sir—I always like that.

"And if you just turn around the way you came, and forget you ever saw me, then nobody has a problem, right?"

He scowled at me. His lips, framed by stubble, were full and very pink.

"They're looking for you."

No kidding. "Uh-huh."

"Did you kill him?"

"What are they saying?"

"Guy taken away in an ambulance. Cops all over the Starlight."

"That so."

"Said you did it."

"Me?"

"Yeah." He frowned again.

"What else they saying, Kenny?"

"Said you're armed and extremely dangerous."

"You'd better believe it."

"There's a posse out hunting for you."

"A what?" I know New Hampshire's not always the most liberal state in the union, but a *posse*? What next? A lynch mob?

"Group of guys left town this morning." He looked at his watch. "'Bout four hours ago."

Four hours? Shit! "Which way they go?"

"Don't worry, man. They went north, figured you drove out of town that way. Police have set up road blocks." He smiled, flashing those crooked teeth at me. "They ain't gonna find nothing though."

"That's right, Kenny."

"They don't know where to look."

"And you do. Clever boy."

"Found your car."

Little bastard. What was I going to do? Break his pretty neck? I could hardly afford to pick up another passenger, however nice a contrast he made to Jody, however much I liked the idea of both of them slobbering over my prick.

"I very much doubt that," I said.

"Silver Chevy Malibu," he said, and rattled off the license number.

"That's not my car."

He seemed to expect this, and just carried on. "If

you think about it, there's only one place in town that a smart guy would hide a car. The dump."

"Uh-huh." I'd run through my repertoire of noncommittal noises.

"Happened before. Guy last year, stole a car down in Boston, drove it all the way here before he gave up. Parked out back of the scrap yard. I guess people think nobody goes there."

I could carry on pretending he was wrong, but where was that going to get us? The kid had information on me, and I had to contain it. "Okay. Very good. Very smart, Kenny. So you found the car and then of course you followed us up here."

He tapped the side of his head. "I just thought about what I'd do if I wanted to get out of the way. Get up on the mountain."

"Right." I thought I'd been clever, but a 19-year-old country boy outsmarted me. "What took you so long?"

Sarcasm was wasted. "Didn't want anyone to follow me. Waited till they were out of town."

"Why didn't you go with them?"

"Oh, they don't want me." He looked down at his bitten nails. "Nobody wants me."

A faint light was dawning in my mind. "What'd they tell you about me, Kenny?"

"Told you. Armed and dangerous."

I nodded back toward the cabin. "What about Jody?"

"That his name? Your boyfriend?"

"Yes." I didn't deny the details, just held his gaze. His eyes were pretty, as big and round as Bambi's, and those eyelashes...

"They said…" He kicked the ground. "Usual bullshit."

"And you just thought you'd come up here on your own, unprotected, and make a citizen's arrest. Was that your big plan?"

"No." He was blushing. My suspicions were correct.

"What is this, then?"

"They call me those names, too. Stuff they said about you and…" He paused, and whispered, "Jody."

"And are they right, Kenny?" I took a step toward him; he didn't back away.

"Maybe."

"I see."

The forest was quiet—a bird singing somewhere in the distance, nothing else but the blood in our heads, the whisper of the air.

"When I want to disappear, I come up here," he said. "Nobody bothers me. My old man and his buddies use the cabin in the hunting season, but all they do is drink beer and tell dirty stories." He looked disgusted. "Shoot a few squirrels. My dad's a jerk."

"And what do you do up here, Kenny?"

"Nothing." He looked cautious.

"Ever bring a buddy?"

"No."

"Ever think about it?"

"Sure, if I had one."

So the lonely gay boy watched his daddy's friends ride out of town, then tracked us down in his own way. Why? To warn us? To get a piece of the action, maybe ride into the sunset with us? To sneak a peek at something he'd never had?

"What are you going to do now, Kenny?"

"I don't know."

"You going to tell the cops what you found?"

He shrugged, looked up at me. He wanted something, but he didn't know how to ask for it.

"We can work something out." It sounded unbelievably corny, but subtlety can waste time. The posse could be riding back into town right now, and if they noticed Kenny was gone someone was might decide to take a look at the old hunting cabin.

"Yeah?"

"You keep your mouth shut about what you saw," I said, "and you can suck my dick."

The words fell like stones in still water. Ripples of emotion traveled across Kenny's face.

"For real?"

"Sure." I squeezed my crotch through the thin fabric of my shorts. "If that's what you want." Not such a big "if." At the age of nineteen, despite all the bullshit I'd put myself through, I'd have sold state secrets to Saddam for a taste of cock.

Kenny was no different. He licked those full pink lips and picked at his pants. "I want it."

"But you better promise me."

"All right! Anything!"

I stepped toward him, took his jaw in my left hand. "Promise you won't tell."

"I promise." He started sucking my thumb.

"Because if you do…"

"Please," he said. "Let me."

"Okay, buster." I stood back, hands on my hips, my dick already pushing its way forward. "It's all yours."

Kenny wasn't the world's most accomplished

cocksucker—the holder of that title was sleeping soundly in the cabin—but he sure was eager, and for those of us who like to see a cute face looking up with lips stretched around the widest part of the shaft—well, this was the jackpot. I ran my fingers through his dark brown curls, pushing his cap to the forest floor, then grabbed hold and eased him downward until he gagged. He brushed tears from his eyes with one grease-stained hand, leaving a black smear on his cheek. He wanted to do everything at once—suck my cock, lick my balls, play with my tits, play with my ass, kiss me, rim me, everything he'd watched online and never managed to do in reality.

I'm a great believer in doing one job at a time and doing it properly. Time for a little old-school discipline.

"Hey! Quit that," I said as he attempted to get both my nuts into his mouth. "Suck my cock, boy."

That had the desired effect. He took a deep breath, opened wide and took it like a man, all the way to the base. I held him there for a while before letting him back off and catch his breath. And then, like all good cocksuckers, he settled into a rhythm. Nice and slow, savoring every mouthful, imprinting the sensation on his memory for repeated playback, eager for the prize but reluctant to end the game.

One hand was ferreting around inside his coveralls.

"Get it out, Kenny. I want to see you."

He stood up, unbuttoned all the way down and shucked the top half. His body was lean and firm, furry in all the right places, with a tattoo on the right-hand side of his stomach. His tits poked through the hair on his chest. It was too much to resist. I pinched them hard;

he closed his eyes and sighed. I put a hand on his ass and pulled him in; he was so hairy back there I thought he was wearing underpants. I was going to have to come back to the White Mountains some time, find this furry little critter and fuck him hard.

But for now, concentrate on the job in hand. Or rather mouth.

He wriggled the grubby denim over his slim hips, letting his cock bounce free, then dropped to his knees again and started sucking. This was not going to take long for either of us. I watched his mouth stretching, saliva running down his chin, his cheeks suctioned in, his fist pumping his dick.

"Look at me, boy."

He turned his eyes up, tears running unchecked down his cheeks, and that did the trick. I started coming, shooting into his mouth. He choked once when he realized what was happening, but held on like a man. His fist was a blur, white jets flying out to sizzle on the carpet of pine needles.

Kenny left the way he came, silent and surefooted down the mountain paths, with a grin on his face, promises that he'd say nothing, and a belly full of semen. Yeah, only a short while ago I was shaking my fist at heaven, telling whoever was listening that I was going to survive, that I was going to protect the man I loved, the violins were soaring and the camera was panning out to show a brave man in a majestic wilderness, the usual widescreen crap. And now I'd fucked the first cute face that came along while Jody was asleep a few yards away. Very noble, Dan. Very heroic. Wow, what a role model you are. What an inspiration.

On an operational level, however, it was justified; Kenny knew where we are, and I'd taken steps to secure his silence.

Sounds good, right? *That blow job was operationally justified.* Try it some time.

I went back to the cabin. Jody was still asleep. If Kenny was as good as his word—and judging by the fuss he made over my dick, he seemed sincere—we were safe for a couple of hours before we continued on foot. Time for him to rest some more, then discuss tactics. Find out if there was anything more that I needed to know. Like, for instance, why exactly Julian Marshall was trying to kill him and frame me.

Jody was cute, Jody was adorable, but Jody had been a hustler since he was fourteen years old, and I guess he found it hard to tell the truth. Even to me. He'd lied about the hit on 54th Street, and for all I knew he was lying still. Trey Peters? Marshall's promise of leaving his wife and playing house with Jody? It could all be a fairy tale. I looked down at his sleeping face, the lips parted, a tear gathering at the corner of the eye, and I thought—it's a mask. He's holding out. There's something in that head that I need to access. Operational information.

Once a marine, always a marine.

I climbed into the bed, put my arms around him and felt that fine, slim body pressing against me as he woke. "Hey, Dan." He sounded happy and relaxed, as if we were on holiday. "What time is it?" He pushed the hair out of his eyes.

"About four in the afternoon. Time to get up, Sleeping Beauty."

He wriggled his butt against me. "Not yet."

"'Fraid so, Jody. C'mon." I pulled the covers back and sat up. "Things to do."

"Oh." He looked around. "I remember." He put his hand to his forehead, felt the bump where he'd walked into that tree. "Shit."

"Are you hungry?"

"Yeah." He sounded depressed.

"Okay." There were some canned goods in the cabin, and plenty of water. I could rustle up something and call it breakfast.

"Are we safe?"

"For now."

"What happened?"

"What do you remember?"

He got out of bed and went to the door. "Jesus. We're in the woods."

"Very good."

"The motel. That guy. You…"

"Yeah."

"Not a dream then." He rubbed his face. "It's not fair. The bad stuff never is."

"Franks and beans okay?"

He pulled a face, then smiled. "If you're cooking it, it's fine."

After a bit of fiddling I lit the stove, opened a can, got busy. Under different circumstances, this would be my idea of the perfect holiday—simple pleasures, nobody to bother us, fresh air, silence. Relocate me several hundred miles to the west—up in Washington State or

Wisconsin or somewhere—and I'd be happy. Here in the White Mountains, our security was compromised.

I needed more information.

"Here you go." I put the pan on the cabin steps and handed him a spoon. We passed it between us, mouthful after mouthful, chewing in silence. When Jody had scooped up the last of the beans, he wiped his mouth on the back of his hand and kissed me on the mouth.

"That was good."

"Thanks."

"What now?"

"Talk."

"Yeah." He sighed, slumping forward. "Thought as much."

"Is there anything you need to tell me, Jody? Any details you've forgotten about?"

"What kind of thing?"

"Like—I don't know." *Like why Julian Marshall the Second is trying to kill you.* "Stuff you don't understand. Things people might have said." I didn't point out that I've been trained in interrogation techniques. Jody's not that up on current affairs or recent history. Not sure the words "Abu Ghraib" mean much to him.

"There's a lot I don't understand." He looked sideways at me, gauging my reaction.

"Let's take it one piece at a time."

"I don't know how anyone knew we were in that motel."

"Okay."

"And I don't know why we haven't gone to the police."

"Don't you?"

He stared out at the trees. "Was that a rat?"

"That was a chipmunk."

"Cute. Never seen one of..."

"Anything else?"

"No. I don't know what you want me to say."

"The truth, Jody. The whole truth."

If at this point he'd put his hand on my leg and started licking his lips to distract me, I might have walked away and left him, even after everything we'd been through. If he's using sex to distract me, to lie to me—well, he's done a damn good job so far. But now the game has changed. If he's worth anything at all, he'll know it.

He said nothing, stared out into the trees.

After a minute he said, "I fucking hate the countryside."

I nodded.

"I want to go home."

"Uh-huh."

"But I don't have a home, do I?"

Silence again, then he looked me right in the eyes. "Ask me some questions."

"Okay. Who knew we were booked into the Starlight Motel in Lincoln, New Hampshire?"

"The guy on the desk."

"Sure."

"The waitress."

"Maybe. Did we tell her?"

"Can't remember."

"Who else?"

He paused, then nodded. "Ferrari."

"Exactly. Ferrari."

"Shit."

"And why haven't we gone to the police, Jody?"

"Because you killed that guy?"

"Maybe, maybe not. But that's not the reason, is it?"

"Because you're afraid of the police."

"Not particularly. But in this case..." I nodded my head. "Maybe."

"What have you done?"

"Me? Nothing much. Illegal firearms, I guess. The rest I can explain. I'm one of the good guys."

"Good for you."

"And you, Jody? Are you one of the good guys?"

His shoulders heaved up and down, and he put a hand over his face. I gave him a minute—but they were getting precious now. If Kenny had a fit of post-swallowing remorse, he could have run back to town, raised the alarm—*there's queers in them thar hills!*—and the posse could be lumbering up the mountain tracks with cops and guns and dogs.

"No."

"What do you mean?"

"I'm no good. I'm a piece of shit." Tears were running down his face, snot bubbling out of his nose.

"Why?"

"I've lied to you."

A cold little voice in my head said *I told you so.* "I know. About the hit man..."

"Not just that. About the deal I did with Marshall." He blew his nose, wiped his eyes. "After Trey Peters died, I didn't hear from Marshall for a while—that was true. But it was him who called me into the office, and told me I had to get out of town to avoid a subpoena."

I whistled. "Who from?"

"The State's Attorney."

"That explains why we were sent up here, then. Out of state."

"Yeah. And I said I'd do it at a price."

"You tried to bargain with him, after what he'd done to Peters?"

"I knew he was scared. I knew too much. I wasn't just some dumb kid."

"And what did you ask for?"

"Money and security. If I agreed to go out of town with a bodyguard to make sure that nobody could get to me—and to make sure that I didn't sneak off and call the State's Attorney—Marshall would set me up with a house and an income for life. He showed me the deed of the place he was going to give me. Upper West Side. Ferrari gave me the cover story to tell you, and he said that if you started asking too many questions I was to...distract you."

"By letting me fuck you?"

"Yeah."

They'd done their homework, then. They knew all about me: my service record, and the reason why it ended. They chose their man well. "So you were supposed to stay out of the way, keeping me happy, until you went back to New York City to claim your prize. Is that it?"

"Yeah."

"And you believed him?"

"I thought I'd been clever."

"And now?"

"I'm not so sure."

"You can say that again."

"Things didn't work out the way I expected, did they? Someone tried to kill me. But before that...I'd already started to... You and me... Shit. It's too late for that now, isn't it?"

I wanted to put my arms around him, to say *it's not too late, we still have a chance, we can make it...*

All the movie lines. But the words wouldn't come out of my mouth. Everything he'd told me so far was a lie; how much more would the story change? Stirling McMahon, Jody Miller—how many skins to this onion? Could I ever trust him, the way I'd trusted Will—with my life? Because that was the game we were in now—life or death. Deep in enemy territory, with hostile agents on our tail.

"Clean yourself up," I said, and my voice sounded gruff. "We've got to move on."

He washed and dressed himself like a man in a daze while I packed up our few belongings.

The time for talk was over. We headed down the mountain as quickly as we could, carrying water and a few provisions, not enough to slow us down. I chose the western slope, the setting sun flashing between the treetops—that way we might slip away before the good burghers of Lincoln returned from their fruitless lynching mission, and we could pick up some kind of transport that would get us out of New Hampshire by nightfall. There was no point in heading for the Canadian border. If the local cops were in Marshall's pocket, we didn't have a chance; they'd be looking for us, even on the quiet, unpatrolled roads. Better to lose ourselves in the west and put as many miles between us and Lincoln as we could.

Paranoid? Maybe. Fits the profile, right? Gay ex-marine, lived his whole life in the closet, went around the world killing people to order, got busted, grudge against the world, screw loose. I'd prefer to say I was being cautious. Julian Marshall had already arranged one death and made it look like an accident—and perhaps Trey Peters was just one of many business associates who had stood in his way. If the State's Attorney was investigating Marshall, he'd stop at nothing to silence Jody. And now I knew as much as Jody did; I was an equal threat. Perhaps there were other witnesses taking similar road trips to ours. How many would die before Marshall was stopped?

The first attempt on our lives, so carefully set up with those convenient witnesses, had failed. Now they were looking for a second chance.

We were close to the foot of the mountain when I saw the squad car parked up at the end of one of those wide forest roads that are marked up for snowmobile use in the winter. We hid behind a boulder and waited.

The car was empty. We could try sneaking past—and we might be lucky. But for all I knew, four of New Hampshire's finest might be combing the woods right now. Sure, they might be good guys. My suspicions about Marshall's corrupt influence might be completely insane. I'd rather find out at a safe distance.

A crack and a swoosh of branches announced the presence of one cop, pushing through the brush to return to the path. He looked hot and pissed off, a dark wet stain down the back of his black uniform shirt, the sleeves rolled up to the elbow. He looked about 35, 40—my age, more or less, and unlike some of his colleagues he'd kept himself in shape. Broad shoulders, a narrow waist, long legs. Unlike me, he had a full head of light brown hair, damn him.

He was about to open the car door when he heard something—not us, thank god, but someone else coming up the track behind him.

"Excuse me, sergeant."

Now, that voice sounded familiar. The cop peered into the gloom—and yes, here he came in his filthy coveralls, baseball cap turned backward on brown curls, white teeth flashing in a smile. My little pal Kenny the cocksucker.

The cop leaned an elbow on the roof of his car. "What are you doing up here, Kenny?" They know each other in these small towns. "Don't you know there's a criminal on the run?"

"Yeah." Kenny stopped and took his cap off. "I been out looking for him."

"You should go home, son."

"But I seen him."

"You did? Where?"

Shit. He got his mouth fucked, and now he's feeling guilty. Little bastard. I'll come back and pay him back, the goddamn...

"Up there." He pointed north, well away from the direction of the cabin. "Two guys in a silver Chevy, right? Driving out Franconia way."

Well, I'll be damned. He was covering for us.

The cop scratched his head; his armpits were wet. "We had men up there. Must have got past us. What time was this?"

"Hour ago. Hour and a half maybe. See that ski trail?"

The cop squinted into the distance. "Where?"

"Way up there, other side of the peak. That's where the track goes. You can get a car through there, easy. Reckon that's the way they went."

"That so."

The cop moved around to the other side of the car

and radioed into the station. "Got an eyewitness report here," said the cop. "Subjects seen heading north toward Franconia. Silver Chevrolet." He turned toward Kenny. "Hey, did you get the model?"

"Not sure. Impala? Malibu, maybe? Didn't get a real good look at the back. That's how you tell the difference. I mean, the engines are how you really know, of course, but…"

"Okay, Kenny. That's enough. Hear that? Impala or Malibu, he says. Yeah. Yeah, right, out Franconia way, 'bout an hour, hour and a half ago. Okay. Sure. Will do."

"Anyone else seen 'em?"

"Maybe. They're radioing it out now. Thanks a lot, kid."

"Looks like you been crawling through a briar patch, Pete."

"Yeah." The cop—Pete—brushed his pants. "And I'm sweating like a horse."

"You should do what I do." Kenny pulled open the front of his blue coveralls, exposing that slim, hairy body. "Go commando."

"Hey, you'll get arrested if you walk around town like that."

"I don't go into town much." He perched his ass on the hood of the car, right next to Pete. "You know me. I'm either under an engine or up in the woods." He leaned back, and his tits came into view. Pete turned to face him.

"You shouldn't spend so much time on your own. Don't you have a girlfriend?"

"Nah." Kenny scratched his stomach. "Not interested."

"Why not? Good looking kid like you could be getting laid every night of the week."

Kenny's hand lingered inside his coveralls, stroking a little lower. "Maybe. And what about you, Pete? You got a new lady?"

"One divorce is enough for me." He rubbed his badge. "Married to the force now."

"Seems like we're neither of us getting any, then," said Kenny. "Shame, huh?"

Officer Pete mumbled something that could have been "Yeah," and ran a finger around his collar. If Kenny was telling me the truth about his lack of experience, he certainly seemed to be on a steep learning curve. This was a textbook seduction.

"You know what I always wanted to do?" said Kenny, now openly rubbing his dick.

"Uh...no."

"Make out on the hood of a car."

"Really?"

"Yeah." Kenny lay back. "Really."

You'd have to be made of stone, or that mythical one-hundred-percent-hetero-he-man, to resist such an invitation. Pete was neither.

"Jesus," whispered Jody beside me. "They're going to..." I silenced him with a look, but I didn't move his hand when he started stroking my leg.

Pete stood between the headlights, between Kenny's open thighs, and leaned forward. Their mouths met, and all I could see was the cop's broad back in its damp black cotton covering undulating as he pressed himself into Kenny.

Tempting as it was to stay and watch the show—or

join in—we had just been given an escape route. The eyes of the law were turning north, and if we could slip out to the west, avoiding the town, we had a chance. I tapped Jody on the shoulder—he was practically salivating at the sight of Pete's muscular ass in its black uniform pants—and we ran swift and silent away from the car. The pine needles cushioned our footfalls, and in less than a minute we were out of earshot. I had a momentary pang of jealousy as I thought of Pete the Cop getting Kenny's furry cherry—and then I saw the truck. A dark blue, beat-up pickup pulled up at the end of the pathway, its nose turned toward the forest road. The windows were down and the key was in the ignition.

Was this Kenny's thank-you present?

I didn't have time to think. We got in, I started her up and we drove.

"You're stealing his truck?"

"Sure. Why not?"

"Because he'll report it. Every cop in the county will be looking for the plates."

I had a pretty strong hunch that Kenny wouldn't do anything of the sort, but I didn't explain that to Jody. "You got a better idea?"

He folded his arms and stared out the window as we reached the highway. He seemed cross. Delayed shock, maybe—or just another of his now-familiar bad moods. There was a radio in the truck, so I tuned into a country and western station and drove on toward the state line.

So what's the plan, Dan?

I don't like drifting. I like objectives and route maps.

As we drove west I had only the vaguest idea of getting to Lake Ontario as fast as possible then onward to Buffalo, Cleveland, Chicago and points west. We could pretty much stick a pin in the map. I kind of favored Wyoming or Montana myself, but that's probably because I liked the idea of fucking Jody in the Rockies, making him grow a beard and living like a couple of mountain men. If we didn't have half the cops in the eastern U.S. hunting for us, I might have suggested it. Unfortunately there was that small matter of the assassination attempt in the Starlight Motel, and the growing certainty that I'd been set up as a sacrificial scapegoat by a bunch of unsavory New York scumbags. The only idea I could really concentrate on was payback.

We'd had one lucky break—a horny teenager with a sentimental streak and access to a fleet of old vehicles, who thought that helping a couple of romantic outlaws, one of whom had just fucked his face, justified hampering a police investigation. There are benefits to having a big dick sometimes. It's a shortcut to getting guys like Kenny to fall in love with you. I'd prefer to be loved for my beautiful personality, but when you've only got ten minutes and the cops are at your back, a couple of extra inches does the job quicker.

Now we needed to get somewhere safe. Then, maybe, I'd talk to the police, tell my side of the story and see what they made of it. If the guy in the Starlight Motel had survived that blow to the head with a smartphone, we might be able to do this the right way. If I'd killed him, I'd have to take matters into my own hands. I don't like the idea of being sent to prison pending investigations. I kind of like my liberty. Isn't that what

I spent twelve years of my life fighting for—liberty? Damned if I was going to place it into the hands of cops and lawyers.

Yeah, I was feeling pretty brave as we drove west. Those violins were soaring again, an aerial shot showed the old blue pickup speeding bravely down the road, *when all the odds are against him, one man takes a stand against injustice...*

"I need a crap."

We were driving by a dreary looking strip mall. It was dark now, and the neon and fluorescents looked tacky as hell. But there was a gas station and a Price Chopper, so I pulled in. Perhaps if Jody took a dump and got some food, he might cheer up. There had been no sign of pursuit, and provided we didn't draw attention to ourselves, we should be fine. I figured we'd sleep in the truck—I didn't want to be noticed more than necessary—but a comfort-and-fuel stop was necessary.

I pulled into the gas station. Jody got out and strutted toward the bathroom. A couple of mean-looking guys in hunting jackets and Red Sox caps watched him through narrowed eyes as I filled the tank. Guess they don't see ass of that caliber too often.

I paid, and followed Jody into the john. He was standing at the basin, T-shirt stripped off, washing himself with soapy water.

"Hey."

"Hey." It was the happiest he'd sounded in a while, so after I'd taken care of Nature I joined him. He splashed me, I splashed him, and before long we were horsing around like a couple of jocks in a locker room. The floor was wet, but there was a mop in the corner.

I'd wipe up before we left. We were in a hurry, but a marine is not a slob.

I saw them in the mirror first, standing in the shadows of the entrance, a little lobby between the forecourt and the interior of the bathroom. The overhead bulb had blown so I could see only silhouettes, but that was enough. The two guys in Red Sox caps. They weren't waiting to use the john.

Jody was singing some stupid pop song, lathering up his underarms; his shorts were soaking and see-through, and any minute now he'd pull them off and start washing his ass. My face and chest were wet, water dripping off the matted hair. My bag was within reach, and in it, firearms.

I touched Jody on the arm. "Shh."

He flinched, and looked at me. One glance told him all he needed to know. He backed toward the stalls.

"Well, well, well," said one of the men, stepping into the light. He was short and dark with deep lines down his face and a two-day beard. "What have we here?"

I said nothing, just wiped my hands on a paper towel. If it came to action, I did not want slippery fingers. The second guy flanked his buddy on the right—taller by a good six inches, blond, broad shoulders and huge hands. Too heavy to be fast, but strong as an ox.

Cops? Didn't look like it. More of Ferrari's hit men? Possibly, but the fact that they were waiting outside a random gas station made it unlikely. Assholes, that's all, looking for a fight.

"Looks like a couple of queers," said Beardy. The Ox sniggered.

"We don't want any trouble." I'd already worked

out the quickest way of dispatching them: kick Beardy in the guts, then smash the Ox's head against the tiled wall. A pistol-whipping if they came back for more. I didn't want a fight; I wanted gas and food and clean clothes at a convenient roadside location. I'd talk my way out of it if I could.

"Sometimes trouble just comes looking for you, though, don't it? Shut the door, Hank."

Hank? Jesus, what kind of movie had we stumbled into? Hank—the Ox—pushed a thick steel bolt into place. Not the first time they'd been through this little performance, it seemed.

Beardy thought they had the advantage, and I guess he could be forgiven; we were wet and nearly naked and new in town. Jody certainly didn't look much of a threat. They'd clocked us getting out of the truck and seen enough to figure out that we were "a couple of queers"—Jody's shorts left little doubt on that score.

I wasn't going to make the first move. We could all walk away from this unscathed; it was up to Beardy. He took a step toward me, scratching his chin; it crackled loud. "Nothing to say for yourself, boy?"

Boy? It's a long time since I've been, or even looked like, a boy. Beardy may have been a few years older than me—early forties, perhaps—but this wasn't about age. Any second now he'd start calling us "ladies" or "girls," and then he would have no teeth left.

"No," I said. "Nothing to say." He took another step toward me. Big mistake. He had placed himself within striking distance.

"How 'bout your friend? He had such a pretty singing voice." He made it sound ridiculous: *pwiddy singin voy-uss.* Jody was shivering in the corner. "Is he frightened?" *Izzy fwighden'd?* "Aw. Poor baby."

This was getting kind of boring, and I was ready to punch my way out of it, but I thought I'd give the asshole one last chance to back down. "What do you want?" I said. "I don't have all day."

"I bet you don't," said Beardy, looking me up and down. "Guess guys like you have a lot of cock to suck, huh?"

One false move, buster...

"Why don't you get your boyfriend to suck my buddy Hank's dick for starters?"

So that was their game, a little restroom rape to pass the time. Picking on queers as a way of getting their rocks off without having to admit they were gay themselves. I know the strategy. Seen it in the armed forces often enough. Probably done it myself.

"Get out of here," I said, keeping my voice low, "before I bust your head."

"Wooooh!" A high, mocking sound. Big Hank sniggered again, showing crooked teeth.

"Before you bust my head? Now that ain't very friendly, queer boy." Boy again. Beardy needed to get glasses—if, that is, I decided to leave both his eyes in working order. A quick gouge would have one of them rolling around in the hand basin.

Hank was picking at his crotch. His jeans were loose and worn, but I could see that he was packing some serious meat.

"So what's it to be, ladies?" That was it; he'd crossed the line. "You suck my buddy's dick, or we kick the shit out of you?"

"Don't much like either of those choices.,"

"You don't? Well, that's too bad." Beardy grabbed my wrist; I think he was planning to twist my arm back and bring me to my knees. That's where the old combat training kicked in, and before he knew what was happening his feet were kicked out from under him, he turned 180 degrees through the air and landed on the wet bathroom floor, taking the fall on his left elbow. Nasty place to hit. Fractures easily, and that can really fuck your arm up. I didn't hear a crack; maybe he was lucky.

Hank watched his pal's unscheduled flight and winced as he hit the deck. Beardy was winded and kicked a little as he fought for breath.

"Guess you picked on the wrong ladies," I said.

"Jeez, Bill, you okay?" Hank and Bill—sounds like an old-time vaudeville act, two dumb rednecks, slapstick and song.

"I...I..." Bill was red in the face, wheezing like a man who's had a heart attack. Hank looked frightened.

"Mister, we didn't mean no harm."

"No shit."

"We were just foolin' around."

"This your idea of foolin' around? Threatening guys in toilets?"

He backed toward the door with his hands out in front of him. "Come on, Bill. Let's go."

But Bill was going nowhere. He managed to take a ragged breath, then vomited over the bathroom floor.

"Oh, Christ, Billy, you okay?" Hank was down on his knees beside him. He looked up at me with terror in his eyes. "What you done to him, mister? You near killed him."

"He'll live."

"Bill. Come on, Bill." Hank rocked his buddy's shoulder—probably not the best thing to do to a man in danger of choking on his own vomit, but he meant well. The poor sap had sure fallen in with some bad company. I threw some paper towels down to him.

"Clean him up," I said. "He'll be okay. Now if you don't mind, we'll just finish off and get going."

Hank dabbed Bill's mouth. As soon as Bill was able to speak, he hissed, "Cocksucking bastard." I thought about kicking him in the stomach.

"Shut up, Bill!" said Hank. "He don't mean it, sir." *Sir*—that made a change from "boy" and "ladies."

"Okay, Big Man. You keep old Bill quiet, and we'll all be friends. Come on, Jody. Let's get going."

Bill groaned and sat up, clutching his elbow on one hand, his gut in the other. "Shit, man, what you do that for?"

I squirted some soap out of the dispenser and started lathering it up between my hands. "I don't take too kindly to being threatened and insulted, pal. So you just fuck off like a good little *boy*, and we'll forget it ever happened."

Jody stepped back to the sink and started rinsing the soap off his body.

We needed to get back on the road, but we also didn't want these guys saying anything about meeting two queer out-of-towners at that gas station. A little insurance might do the trick and provide some entertainment in the meantime. "You better get out of those shorts," I said to Jody. "They're wet through."

He caught my eye and did as I suggested, bending

right down to give our would-be assailants a perfect view of his asshole. I took his shorts from him and threw them in Bill's face, where they landed with a satisfying splat. He flinched, but checked himself. He knew when he was beaten.

"Now clean yourself up, kid. Get it all nice and sweet for me. You ever seen a piece of ass as sweet as that, Bill?"

Bill said nothing, just scowled as he wiped his face.

"What about you, Hank? You the ass man?"

Hank smiled. "Uh, yeah. It's a pretty ass."

"So come on, Bill," I said, "what's your position on the team? You like to watch while Hank gets his dick sucked? That how you get off?" I kept my tone friendly. One hostile move from Bill and he'd be singing soprano.

He wheezed, "Fuck you," from the floor, while Hank dabbed bits of vomit off his jacket.

"Fuck me? I don't think so. Now, if you wanted to fuck anyone, you could do a lot worse than my friend Jody here." I ran a hand over his creamy smooth ass. "Best I've had in a long, long while. Wha'd'ya think, Hank?"

Hank was staring, licking his lips, his attention wandering from his stricken friend to Jody's perfect backside.

"He likes to get fucked?"

"You bet. Don't you, Jody?"

"Yeah." Jody caught my tone and wriggled his hips lasciviously. "I love it."

"Sure is pretty." Hank's voice was hoarse. I guess he didn't get much pussy, male or female, without the use of force. He wasn't bad looking—no great conversationalist, that's for sure, but he'd make a serviceable husband.

"Wanna piece?" said Jody, standing over them. He was half hard now; only a minute or two ago he was cowering terrified in the corner of the bathroom. That boy's libido never ceased to impress me.

"Yeah."

"Now hold it just a moment," I said. "We don't want to upset old Bill, do we? He doesn't like queers. Ain't that right, Bill?"

Bill sat on the floor and said nothing.

"Maybe he just never met the right guy," said Jody. "Someone who could show him how." He reached around my waist and undid the top of my shorts. "Like my friend here." He opened my fly and exposed the base of my cock. "He's a very good teacher."

Hank was openly rubbing his crotch. Bill, while not exactly smiling, had stopped scowling.

"It's okay, Bill," I said. "The door's locked, remember? Anything you do is just between the four of us." Jody pulled my prick out and stroked it a few times; it was quickly hard.

"I ain't queer," said Bill.

"And I'm Britney Spears," said Jody, and pulled my shorts down. I felt his hard cock against my hairy ass.

"Tell you what," I said, "I'm willing to cut you guys a deal. You play nicely, you'll walk out of here. Any more of your shit, and you leave in an ambulance." My cock was fully hard now. "What's it to be?"

"Suck him, dude," said Hank. "Come on."

With a decent show of reluctance, Bill hauled himself

to his knees. Maybe he'd been waiting for an opportunity like this, when it wouldn't be his choice, his fault. Maybe he'd been antagonizing queers in gas station restrooms for months, hoping to find someone who'd turn the tables. If so, he'd found what he was looking for. I took hold of his bristly chin and made him look up. He was an ugly fucker compared to Jody, even compared to Hank, who wasn't exactly model material, but underneath that shitheel exterior there was a perfectly good cocksucker just waiting to break out. "Now then, Bill," I said, stroking his lower lip with my thumb, "you're going to suck this dick, and you're going to suck it good. You try to bite me, I break your arm. Understand?"

He looked me in the eye and nodded.

"Good man."

And then he did the thing that convinced me I was right. He closed his lips over my thumb and ran his tongue over it.

He was ready. I let him nurse on my thumb for a moment, then put my hand on the back of his head. He knew what that meant and opened wide. I waved my cock in his face, but he was impatient. He steadied it with one hand and took the head in his mouth. His tongue flicked over my piss slit, and his lips moved down.

It felt good. No awkward blocking with the teeth. He'd done this before, plenty of times, in different bathrooms, perhaps, and with different accomplices.

While I pushed Bill's head down on my dick, Jody was eyeing up the big blond giant. I knew he'd noticed the bulge in Hank's pants, and he wasn't going to let that get away. He put one foot up on the basin, pulled his asscheeks apart and ran a finger around his hole.

Hank got the message loud and clear. He unzipped his pants and pushed them down to his knees. His white cotton shorts were stretched to their breaking point.

"Come on, man," said Jody, "fuck me."

Hank stood up—he was at least six foot four—and pulled the white cotton aside. Out sprang the biggest dick I've seen outside a farm. Jody was not deterred. He picked a condom out of his Dopp kit and handed it to Hank.

"You know what to do with that, right?"

"Oh, sure," said Hank, tearing the packet open with his teeth. "I use 'em with my wife."

I caught Jody's eye, and I guess he wanted to laugh as much as I did. Hank rolled the rubber over his cock and spat into his hand. Jody pushed his ass out and braced himself against the mirror.

Bill, trying to keep an eye on the action while sucking, brushed me with his teeth.

"Hey! Watch it!"

He looked up and mumbled something which might have been "Sorry." I pulled him in and fucked his throat. He didn't gag.

Watching Hank line himself up at Jody's backdoor made me even harder in Bill's mouth. He sensed it and ran his tongue up and down my shaft. "You want it too, man?" He said nothing but just kept sucking, which was a pretty articulate reply. "Okay." I pulled out of his mouth just as Hank pushed into Jody's ass. Jody groaned and tugged on his cock as Hank's big hands ran over his smooth broad back.

"Oh, man," said Hank, sounding surprised. "That is a nice ass."

I pulled Bill to his feet; he was still in pain, but he wasn't complaining anymore. One taste of cock had put him in a much better mood. I turned him around and bent him over the sink.

"Drop your pants."

He did as he was told, presenting a hairy, thickset ass to my view.

"Not bad," I said. "You could stand to lose a few pounds, build up a bit of muscle..." I slapped him, hard, but he didn't complain. "But not bad at all."

I rolled one of my ever-present condoms over my cock and slicked it up with soap from the dispenser. It would sting him, but did I care? To my left, Jody was getting deep into his fuck; his eyes were half-closed, his face and neck flushed. Apart from his trainers and socks he was completely naked. Hank drove that thick tool deep into him with a look of bewildered delight on his face. Perhaps he'd never found an ass that could take him before.

Bill, meanwhile, was as easy to break into as Fort Knox. I pressed my head against the hole—nothing doing. I pressed harder, and it was like trying to fuck a tennis ball. Perhaps he'd had second thoughts. I reached around and felt his dick—it was hard. I took that as permission to continue—not that I needed it.

"Take a deep breath," I said, "and relax. And now"—I felt him yield—"breathe out."

On the out breath his ass suddenly opened, and I glided in. Not all the way—I was feeling charitable—but far enough to make him groan with pain. He bit into his forearm. I stopped for a while, waited for him to get used to it and then, when a little wiggle in his rear gave me the green light, I fed him the second half.

"All right!" said Hank, who was pumping in and out of Jody like a machine. "My buddy Bill's getting a dick up his ass!"

I guess it needed to be said. Bill grunted, "Yeah," and opened further. I started fucking him properly, taking my tempo from Hank. Soon we were in sync. I had no doubt about whose dick was getting the better treatment, but there was something about putting this bully in his place that was working on me like Viagra. Okay—not a nice thing to feel, but I'm not a nice person. I like power. It turns me on. Blame the USMC.

"I wanna turn over," said Jody. "I wanna see you."

Hank pulled out, and Jody lifted himself up on to the sink surround. He raised his legs, scooted forward and presented his hole at dick level. Hank took advantage of the break to remove his jacket and shirt. His torso was huge, solid and covered in blond fur.

"How 'bout you, Billy Boy? Want to look me in the eye while I fuck you?"

I didn't need to suggest it twice. Within moments, my only concern was whether the chipboard sink unit could sustain the weight of two men getting fucked. I positioned the head of my cock at Bill's ass, and his hand guided it in.

We got back into rhythm, and all that was left to decide was who was going to come first.

You won't be surprised to learn that it was Bill. His fist came down to his cock and started working it, leaking all over his belly—so much, in fact, that I thought he'd already shot his load—but he remained hard. From the way he was groaning, it wouldn't take long.

One big blob of cum appeared at the head of his dick and spread over his hand.

"Look at that," I said. "Bill's popping his nuts while I fuck him up the ass."

The second lot shot out at force, hitting Bill on the chin and landing in a line down his shirt and stomach. A third and fourth added to the mess.

It looked like Hank was going to take the silver medal, from the way his pace was picking up. But then inspiration struck.

I pulled out of Bill's ass, removed the condom and threw it in the sink. Relieved, he lowered his legs and stood up.

"Not finished with you yet, *boy*," I said. "On your knees."

He looked puzzled, but his still-hard cock was doing his thinking for him. He obeyed.

"Come on, guys," I said. "We're going to give old Bill here something to remember."

Hank pulled out of Jody and we stood around Bill, three hard dicks jerking in his face, slapping his cheeks—which, given the bristles there, was kind of painful—and rubbing against his lips.

Jody was the first to let go, and the force of his load surprised me until I realized that Hank had a couple of thick fingers up his ass. All of it sprayed into Bill's face. He screwed up his eyes but didn't close his mouth. When Jody had finished, Bill swallowed and licked his lips.

I was next, adding another thick layer to Bill's stubble and some more to swallow.

Hank's brawny arm was working on his tool, and he

was making so much noise that anyone standing outside must have heard him. Jody couldn't keep his hands to himself, and so he grabbed Hank's cock, pointed it toward Bill's face and delivered the last few strokes. Hank bellowed, shooting so much jizz that Bill's face was almost invisible under the viscous coating. When he'd finished—and it took a while—Bill took Hank's cock in his mouth and sucked it.

It was a touching finale.

Jody and I washed up and left the two of them on the sticky bathroom floor. It took a lot of wiping before Bill was able to open his eyes and struggle shakily to his feet; by that time we were both dressed.

"Thanks for the fuck, guys," I said, shouldering my bag.

"Yeah," said Hank, grinning like an idiot. Bill looked shamefaced, insofar as that's possible when you have cum drying in your hair and dripping off your chin.

Buffalo, Cleveland, Chicago, the west...

That's what I said. Wasn't it? Well, we made it as far as Buffalo.

Jody mellowed out after our little bathroom interlude. Any jealous suspicions he'd been harboring about Kenny seemed to have been soothed by ten inches of Viking dick up his ass. As for me, I'm not the jealous type. Never had the chance to be. Maybe if I'd seen another officer making a move on Will Laurence, I'd have killed him—but at the time my only fear was being found out. And now? How did I feel watching the man I was beginning to love get ploughed in a grungy gas station? Pass. Next question. It's hard to feel jealous when your dick's up someone else's ass. The only regret I had was that we'd wasted time. I don't like digressions. I like to stick to the plan. What happened back there was gratuitous.

But hell, we might both die tomorrow.

We drove for hours, well into the night. I should have been tired—Jody was asleep within twenty minutes—

but I was wide awake, and while I felt that way I wanted to put a couple of hundred miles behind me. I do my best thinking when I'm driving. I like the distraction of the road, the mechanical business of accelerator and brakes—and, in the case of this old rust-bucket, stick shift. If the practical part of my brain is engaged, the other stuff just works itself out nicely.

I had two objectives: stay alive, and get revenge on the bastards who tried to kill us. The first one was fine; I had a much better chance of survival if I got as far out of Marshall's reach as possible. As for the second—well, I didn't have a fucking clue. What would you do? Get tooled up like Rambo and go blasting into the offices of Marshall Land wearing an oil-stained vest? "Eat lead, motherfuckers," bang, crash, roll credits? Fine, go ahead. But like I said, I have a taste for liberty. I don't want to spend the rest of my life on death row.

So I thought—Chicago. Big city, and I had a couple of old service buddies out that way. People who would put me up for a couple of nights, not ask too many questions—even if I was with Jody. Tough guys, like me. Useful if there was trouble. Talk to the Chicago cops, put Jody under their protection.

Establish base. Consolidate forces. Plan and execute. Textbook stuff.

And then my mind wandered as I drove through the night, heading toward Albany where I'd pick up Route 90. We'd sleep somewhere—a rest area, a parking lot, didn't matter—and set off as soon as I'd found coffee. Probably sounds like hell to some people, but it's familiar territory to me. Roughing it is sleeping in the open, under fire. A truck with doors and seats? Luxury.

What would be better than that? A bed, yeah, okay. A bed and a bathroom and a door with a lock. Peace and privacy. That's what I used to long for when we were out in Afghanistan. Just somewhere we could be alone together—a little hidey-hole big enough for two. We managed it a few times. Twice, to be precise, and although the door would have come down with one good kick of an MP's boot, and the walls were so thin that you could hear the TV in the next room, it was good enough for us.

Will and me.

The memory hit me in the guts like a punch, and the taillights of the car ahead got blurred. Shit? Was it raining? Must be. Can't be tears.

Will—so beautiful, as he lay naked on the tacky bedspread of that cheap hotel in Kabul. Yes, seriously, Kabul. That's where we went on our furlough. We didn't want to waste time traveling, and we didn't want to hang out with the guys. We found a place where the U.S. dollar would buy us a bit of privacy—a small room on a noisy street with dirty walls and a nylon bedspread, and in that miserable setting Will Laurence shone like a fucking diamond. His skin was smooth and brown, his body firm and warm, and he looked up at me as I stood over him, one hand behind his head, the other playing with his balls, and he said, "Fuck me, Dan. Fuck me."

Tonight that warm, brown body lies in a cold cemetery in Knoxville, Tennessee, mourned by family and friends. Not me. No, sir. Not invited to the funeral. They probably never knew I existed. Why should they? After all, what did it amount to? Furtive fucks on military bases, a couple of nights in a Kabul fleapit, a lot of implausible bullshit spoken under the stars by perimeter fences.

A sniper's bullet put an end to that.

Jesus Christ, my head hurt. I pinched my brow, just above the nose. Too many unshed tears. Time to stop the car, pull over, get some sleep. And hope I don't dream. I can't stand waking up when I've dreamed that he's alive.

I turned off into a little town, quiet streets, not even a cop car or a dog sniffing the lamp posts. There was a church up the way with an empty parking lot. That would do. Jody stirred when I turned off the engine. There were a couple of blankets on the backseat—considerate Kenny—and we improvised a bed. Of course Jody wriggled his butt against me and tried to get his hand in my pants, and although my dick was hard I was too tired and too sad to do anything about it.

I wish I had. Because the next day I lost him.

Everything was fine until we got to Buffalo. That's a long, hard drive down Route 90, stopping only for fuel, and there were times when I didn't think the truck would make it. I had to change the oil around Rochester, which took too long; Jody went for a walk while I talked engines with the slob who ran the garage. But we were back on the road in twenty minutes, heading west, and we were both excited. Jody sat in the passenger seat with his feet on the dash, drumming on his thighs, singing and talking nonsense—someone had too much sugar and caffeine in his diet. But it was good to see him cheerful after the rollercoaster moods of the last couple of days. Once this was all behind us, I'd get him up into the woods and mountains, wean him off junk food and cosmetics, and make him into the man I wanted him to be.

Pathetic, right? A middle-aged man trying to turn a young hustler into the husband he's always dreamed of. But it was a nice idea, and it took my mind off my troubles. I was feeling pretty happy when we pulled into the motel parking lot. I figured we were far enough from potential danger to rent a room. Marshall's influence couldn't possibly extend this far. What could he do? Call up every single motel in the United States? We hadn't been followed or stopped. There was no interstate police manhunt. We'd slipped through the net, and we deserved clean sheets and hot running water. And I kind of felt like I owed him a fuck from last night. The blues had passed, and I was already thinking about just how I was going to do him. And maybe...well, maybe I'd let him have a turn on top. The idea excited me. In fact, my ass was tingling as I carried the bags into our room, and mine is an ass that doesn't tingle often. Jody had gone up the street to buy the essentials. We'd passed a Target on the way in, where he could pick up some clean underwear for us both and a fresh supply of rubbers.

I badly wanted a shower, but I waited for Jody to get back. We could save water by showering together. I always like to consider the environment.

Target must have been busy. Half an hour went by, and that tingle in my ass was starting to turn into a niggling anxiety. Had something happened to Jody? Had he run off and left me? He'd been nervous and excitable in the truck; maybe he was making plans of his own. How well did I really know him, after all?

He'd lied about so much—his name, his history, his relationship with Julian Marshall—maybe he was lying still. Maybe this whole crazy road trip was a charade. Maybe I was being set up as an accessory to something else. See, love and trust don't necessarily go together in my book. How long had I known Jody? A few days, that's all. Sex, danger, hours on the road—how well do you really get to know someone?

I put my shirt back on and hesitated at the door. Should I take a gun? I'd hidden them away under the bed; surely nothing could happen between here and Target that would need a weapon. Calm down, Dan. You're an ordinary guy going to pick his boyfriend up from the store. You do not need to go in armed.

I locked the door, smiled and shook my head. There was the old blue pickup, the hood still warm. Five or six other vehicles in the lot. Traffic on the road. A bus. A truck. A normal evening in the suburbs of Buffalo, New York.

I walked toward the store. It was a nice evening. Fuck first, then maybe find a beer and a burger. Then more fucking.

And there in the distance, maybe fifty yards away, was Jody, a plastic bag slung over his shoulder.

A car pulled up at the side of the road and crawled along beside him, walking pace. My heart tripped quickly, and suddenly all my senses were alert. A dirty old man, maybe, or a bunch of drunken thugs looking for a queer to bash?

Come on. This was just someone asking for directions. The car stopped, Jody leaned through the window and spoke to someone inside. He pointed up the road, talked some more, nodded. See? Perfectly simple explanation. Nothing sinister, nothing dangerous. Not every street is a war zone.

The curbside rear door opened and a man jumped out, grabbed Jody's arm, twisted it behind his back and pressed his head down. Jody was bundled into the backseat, the door slammed, and I saw a brief flash of flailing limbs as the car sped away, tires squealing.

If I'd had a gun I might, just might, have got a bullet into one of the rear tires. As it was, all I could do was watch helplessly as the car receded into the distance. Not even a chance of getting the license plate. Can you describe the vehicle, Major Stagg? It was black. That's about it. A black car. How many of them are there on the road?

I counted another fourteen as I walked back to the motel.

Kidnapped. Abducted. Quite possibly dead by now—shot in the head in the back of the car and dumped by the road. If they know what they're doing, he might not be found for weeks. People don't come walking along the busy roads. People don't notice things like clouds of flies or bad smells. And who's going to report Jody Miller missing?

Only me.

So what was I waiting for? Why was I sitting on the edge of the bed—the bed where I'd hoped to take a dick up my ass for the first time in many years—rocking backward and forward and struggling with the feeling that I'd been set up?

How did I know that they hadn't waited until I came looking for Jody before they staged the heist? What had he been doing in the half hour he was absent? What had he done earlier, when we stopped for oil in Rochester?

Who had he talked to? Who had he called?

The U.S. Marine Corps prepares you for many things, but it also makes you very suspicious. You question everything. Being a lawyer might be worse, but only just. Now most people, if they'd seen a friend or a lover being bundled into the back of a mysterious black car after there had already been two attempts on his life would have panicked, called the cops or at least given chase. Not Dan Stagg. Dan Stagg sat there figuring out strategy and counter-strategy as if he was dealing with an Al-Qaeda cell, not a flaky hustler and a couple of New York sleazeballs.

Ten minutes went by. Fifteen, and I didn't move. Jody is dead, or the whole thing is a setup and he's still lying to me. Either way, I've lost him. You're alone again, Dan, just the way you like it, just the way you deserve. The only love you've ever known is in a grave in Tennessee, a grave you dare not visit, and now—hey! You're free! You've got wheels and the remains of those ten-thousand bucks, and there's a great big country out there for you to kill yourself in.

I lay back on the bed and stared at the ceiling. Another goddamn light fixture, another fan, another motel room on another road, around and around and around we go, where we're going no one knows...

What the fuck? Jody has been abducted, and I'm wasting time on self-pity? Me, the big Marine Major, sulking like a teenager. I went to the bathroom, splashed water on my face and stared in the mirror. I lost one to a sniper in Afghanistan—was I going to lose another to a gangster in New York? Why was I trying to convince myself that Jody was lying? Because I wanted it all to end, to return to the half-life I'd been living before he came along? Because it was easier, less painful, less real…

Was I going to creep back to New York with my dirty money and hide? And what about the dreams—could I deal with them? Not just Will now, but Jody, too. The ones I lost. The ones I let down.

You have a choice, Stagg, I said to my reflection in the mirror. You can believe he's lying, and you can sink into the shit. Or you can have a little faith, and do what you know is right. You can give up on life, or you can fight.

And the old marine training kicked back in.

Analyze. Assess. Act.

There was only one course of action. Gather information—track Marshall and Ferrari—find Jody. And I couldn't do that by sitting on my ass in Buffalo. I needed to get back to the City. I'd go as far as I could in the truck, and when that broke down I'd hitch a ride or take a bus. I had money, I had firearms and, best of all, I had an objective.

Save Jody Miller.

Twelve hours later I was lying on the bench-press machine in my local Harlem gym wondering what to do next. I'd phoned every shady character I could think of, from hustlers and pimps all the way down to lawyers and journalists, looking for leads on Marshall Land. Did they know anything about Trey Peters? Had they heard of a character calling himself Enrico Ferrari? Yes, they'd heard things. Julian Marshall was under investigation by the State's Attorney for blackmail, extortion, suspected murder. And did they know about disappearing witnesses? There were rumors. They'd make inquiries and call me back. And that, I concluded, was that. All I could do was wait.

So I racked up the weights and bench-pressed. The gym was quiet: too early for the club crowd, too late for the working crowd, just me and a couple of older guys pottering around the machines, minding our own business.

"Want me to spot for you?"

Hmm—not minding our own business quite enough. I looked up and saw one of my regular admirers, a grey-haired guy at least ten, fifteen years older than me, not in bad shape for his age, but a little too fond of hanging around the showers pretending to wash while sneaking a peek at the guys. Sometimes I've been glad of the attention, to be honest.

"Sure."

What the hell, give the guy something to jerk off to later, when he goes home to his wife or his TV dinner or whatever. I hoisted the weight and let the bar hover around his hands before lowering it slowly to my chest. A few more reps—six, seven, eight—and I was ready for him to take it. That should give him time to feast his eyes on my arms, chest, legs, whatever.

"Haven't seen you for a while," he said, as I sat up and wiped my face.

It was kind of comforting to know that one person at least in New York City noticed my absence. "I've been working."

"Good to see you back."

"Thanks, man." I strolled over to the water cooler; he followed me.

"What's your line of work?"

"This and that," I said. "Been doing a bit of personal security."

His eyebrows flickered upward. "Nice." He smiled.

"And you?" I had no real desire to engage him in conversation, but I do have some basic manners. "What do you do?"

"Oh, I'm semiretired now," he said, scratching his grey beard. "Still do a few jobs for the old firm."

"And what was that?"

"I'm a lawyer."

I nodded. "That so?"

"Yeah."

I drank, he drank.

"What sort of stuff?"

"Criminal, mostly."

"Mmm-hmm." He was starting to look more interesting. "White-collar?"

"Yeah. Did a few high-profile RICO cases back in the day." He laughed. "That's a great way to make enemies."

"I bet." I wonder...I just wonder... "Well, I'm done for now. Think I'll hit the steam room."

"Okay."

"You coming?"

His face lit up. "Sure. Great idea."

"Right." In the locker room I stripped and headed for the shower, pretty sure that he'd follow. He did.

My gym is one of those old-fashioned places

untouched by twenty-first-century prudery—three chrome showerheads sticking out of the wall, no cubicles or dividers, just a wall of white tile, tolerably clean. The water was hot and strong, and at least one of the dispensers had soap in it. I picked the right-hand shower and got washing.

He took the left-hand one. I wondered what excuse he'd find to move to the middle.

By the time I'd washed my face and got the soap out of my eyes, he was standing under the water facing me, one hand against the wall, the other pulling his foot up for a quad stretch. How many times, I wondered, did he go through this routine? How many casual conversations on the gym floor were followed by hopeful trip to the showers? Oh, well—it was nice to be admired. And he wasn't bad looking, for an old guy. I mean, one day I'd be that age…

And then I saw it. It was semifluffed, not quite hanging straight down. Next to his bent leg it looked like a slightly smaller extra limb. I did a double take, stared for a moment then realized what I was doing. He didn't miss it. I guess he was used to it.

"I did legs today," he said, sounding very matter-of-fact. "Feeling a bit creaky." He swapped legs, and his meat flopped around a bit, a stream of water shooting off the end. "At my age, you don't snap back into shape quite so quick."

"You look pretty good to me."

"Thanks." He put his foot down and ran a hand along his stomach. There was a bit of flesh on it, but only a bit. An inch or so under the surface there was muscle. "Too many guys of my age just give up."

"And mine." I copied his gesture, running my hand over the wet hair on my ridged stomach. That touch was all it took—my dick started soaring, from zero to forty-five degrees in ten seconds.

Now it was me who was looking for an excuse to move to that middle shower.

I'd like to say I struggled with my conscience at this point, that I thought of Jody and our future together, took a deep breath and walked out of that shower with my dignity intact. But I've never claimed that I'm a good person, a nice person or even a particularly honest person. I wanted that cock, I wanted to submit to him, and if there's one thing you learn during twelve years in the USMC, it's how to submit to your seniors.

"Shit," I said, making some feeble play with the perfectly well-equipped dispenser, "soap's out." I reached across, preceded by my penis which was now pointing toward him like a diviner's rod.

I washed my chest, arms and legs while he went through a few more basic stretches, watching me with a half-smile. I turned around and washed my ass, making sure he got a good look. He obviously did. When I turned back, his cock was starting its own journey northward. I don't know how, but that monster got thicker and longer, and by the time it was nearing the horizontal it looked like something you might throw on the fire.

"What's your name?" His voice sounded gruff.

"Dan."

"You a hooker, Dan?"

I almost laughed, which would have been tactically disastrous.

"No, sir."

"Security guard?"

"Ex-marine." I don't know why I told him that. I think I was hypnotized.

"So, we going to get some steam?" He nodded toward a glass door at the end of the room.

"Sure."

"At least it's private." He held the door for me.

The steam room was probably once a mop cupboard, converted with a couple of benches and a vaporizer so that the gym could add the word "spa" to its title. It smelled of eucalyptus oil and wasn't so much steamy as humid, but I didn't care. The only feature that really interested me was the door.

He closed it behind him. What with him and me and his dick makes three, there wasn't much room to turn around. That suited us just fine. He stepped up behind me, put one arm around my waist and the other around my chest, and pulled me in. His left hand found my right tit, his right hand found my cock, and that third leg pressed right up against my ass. Jesus, I thought, feeling the size of it, I may not be walking out of here. But at that moment, mobility seemed a small price to pay.

"You want me to fuck you, boy?"

In answer I shoved backward. He kissed my neck and I twisted my face around to meet him. He kept pinching and jerking as our tongues touched. His arms were strong around me, turning me to face him, our dicks jousting below the waistline. I was stubbly as hell, which didn't seem to be a problem. His hands shifted, one to the back of my head, the other to my ass. I'm surprised that it didn't get sucked in; I felt like I had a vacuum cleaner inside me, and someone had just switched it on to max. He broke the kiss, moved back half a pace and took both our cocks in his hand, stretching thumb and forefingers to press them together, shaft to shaft, side to side. I looked down, saw his dwarfing mine, half as big again, maybe more. I'm not one of those men who judges everything by size, but I'm kind of used to being the larger party. Now, I felt small. And you know what? I liked it. The contrast turned me on. I wished, for the first time in my life, that my dick was smaller. I wanted to be completely in his power.

He jerked the two of us in unison. "Think you can take it?"

This was no time for boasting. "I'm not sure. It's been a long time since...you know."

"Okay. We'll start easy." He sat on the bench and patted his thigh. "Sit down, Dan." I did as I was told, and he put an arm around my shoulders. "Now lean back and relax."

My back was half against his chest, half against the wooden wall of the steam room. He ran a hand up and down my wet, furry torso, digging his fingers into my bush, then leaned down and took a mouthful of tit, sucking and gently biting. I sighed and shuddered, and I felt my dick ooze. His cock was pressed between my hip and his stomach.

He put one hand under my thigh and pulled my leg into a bent position, then scooped up my balls and lifted them. "Hold these," he said, as if he was asking me to look after the luggage on a train journey. Well, the train was about to enter the tunnel, that's for sure.

I held on to my balls as he spat on his fingers and worked them around my asshole.

"Take it easy, man," I said.

He kissed me on the mouth and pushed one finger inside me, just to the first knuckle. It felt weird at first, like I was taking a shit—but he knew what he was doing and gave me enough time to get used to it. Then a little further, feeling the resistance giving way, checking that I was still hard—yeah, he was an expert. All the stuff I do when I'm breaking a guy in.

"Good boy."

All the old lines—the lines I've used—but the roles were reversed. I was the boy, he was the daddy, the boss, the master. Half an hour ago—twenty minutes—I was a battle-scarred ex-marine who thought he'd seen it all. Well, I guess you *can* teach an old dog new tricks. When a second finger entered me I grunted, shifted around on his lap and opened up to take it. My dick seemed to get harder. I felt as if I was starting to come, but it was a different sensation—relocated, it seemed, to somewhere deep inside me.

Those two fingers slid in and out, in and out, as he held me with one arm around my shoulders, my head thrown back, my throat exposed, his lips kissing the bristly skin. His fingertips found my prostate gland— no-man's-land for so long I sometimes wondered if it was still there—and started pressing.

I kind of...passed out. Zoned out. I don't know what to call it. New territory. Evaluate. Assess.

Time passed.

"You're ready."

"Huh?" I was incapable of coherent speech. I didn't

need it. My ass was doing the talking for me. I leaned back on the bench and pulled my knees up. I wanted to see him while he fucked me.

"This is going to hurt, Dan."

"I know."

"Sure you want it?"

"Mmm."

That was all the encouragement he needed. He placed a condom over the head of his cock and rolled it down. Confident, he'd come prepared. I didn't even know they made them in his size.

"Cold," he said, rubbing lube around my hole. One finger slipped in, worked around in a circle. Then he got to work on his dick, slicking it up. It took a couple of generous applications to cover the entire rubber-sheathed surface area.

"Tell me if you want me to stop."

"Okay."

"Sure?"

I made a sound which I can't put into letters, mostly at the back of my throat.

He stood over me, stroking his lubed-up dick. How many men really wanted that thing? And how many of those could actually take it? Well, he was in luck. I may not be used to a cock up my ass, but I have extensive military training and know how to endure pain for a worthy objective.

And from where I was sitting, or rather lying, it looked pretty damn worthy to me. I took a deep breath and then, as soon as I felt him push, exhaled.

Jesus Christ. It was like labor in reverse. I screwed up my eyes, bit my lip and tried to breathe through it. Steady, Stagg, steady. You're trained for this. Go through the pain, not under. Focus ahead. Clear the mind. Breathe.

The agony subsided, leaving behind it a warmth that I have never known before. Every muscle in my body seemed to relax. He sensed it, waited a while, caressed my thighs, and then, slowly, gently, advanced. I've made easier advances through enemy territory under heavy fire—he encountered resistance every inch of the way—but the further he got, the easier the going, and finally, to our mutual surprise, his pubic hair hit my balls, and I'd taken the lot. I felt him right up to my guts. I half expected to feel him in my throat.

"You're doing well," he said, as if I was undergoing some kind of operation which, in a sense, I was. "Now, just relax." He took hold of my cock which, to my surprise, had gone completely soft. "Let's see if we can get this hard again. It'll be a lot more fun if we can."

"I feel like I'm going to come."

"Don't worry," he said. "I know what I'm doing."

He did, too. He stroked the underside of my dick with the back of his fingers, gently, until it started to stir. Then he took it by the base between thumb and forefinger and wagged it from side to side, slapping it against my thighs. I could feel the blood flowing back into it, and as it did so the sensation inside my ass got stronger. When it was fully hard, he bounced it against the palm of his hand a few times, testing it.

"You'll do," he said, leaned forward and kissed me on the mouth. At the same time he pulled his dick out a few inches, leaving what felt like an intolerable vacuum inside, and then thrust.

I realized, with that thrust, that I had never really been fucked before. Yeah, I'd let a few guys in—and I'd enjoyed it; it made a change. But I'd never felt what guys like Jody felt—that ecstasy that makes their eyes roll back in the head, that makes them lose it completely, bucking around like a crazy steer. I used to put it down to types: you were a top, or a bottom, and while you might switch around from time to time, you never really changed.

And here was a guy in his fifties in an uptown steam room showing me that everything I ever knew was wrong.

He started slow, which was just as well; I was struggling to keep up. Pain was never far away, lurking just below the surface of this new pleasure. I was either going to scream or come. I checked my dick—still hard. The temptation to grab it and start jerking was enormous, but it would be all over in four strokes. I wanted this to last.

He wasn't one of those guys who likes to keep up a running commentary, thank god; some people watch too much porn and feel the need to put everything into words. One of the best things about sex is that it's nonverbal, and I like to keep it that way. Instructions and requests are fine—and, in this case, the occasional question about one's well-being—but apart from that, I don't need to be told that a dick is up my ass. I can feel it.

After cruising along in first gear for a while, he shifted into second and, when he sensed I was ready, third. Now we were getting somewhere. I caught up with him—I don't know how else to express it. Whereas

before I'd submitted to his cock in my ass, and concen-
trated on not suffering, now I went over some kind of
hump and I wanted everything he could give. I opened
my legs wider, shifted my ass forward and upward to
get maximum thrust. He went into fourth. I heard a
sound—and I realized it was my voice, a low, monoto-
nous groan, louder and softer as he thrust in and out.
I don't know if he was worried about anyone hearing
us—but anyway, he kissed me again, and picked up
speed. We were racing along in fifth, on the freeway,
no traffic, no bumps in the road, just a smooth, fast,
exhilarating ride toward our destination...and it was
getting closer...and closer...

I reached around and felt his balls, felt with a tingle
of shock the thickness of his dick, the circumference my
ass had been stretched to, and then, suddenly, I started
to come.

He must have felt it—felt some stirring inside me—
because he righted himself, grabbed my cock and held
it while the semen shot out, hitting the wall behind me,
my chin, my neck, and finally landing in lines on my
chest and stomach.

I came and came, so long and so hard I stopped being
surprised and just let it take me.

He didn't stop fucking. If anything, he got harder.
For ten seconds, twenty, thirty, a full minute, he kept
fucking my ass until the very last shiver of my orgasm
was over, and then, burying himself deep inside me and
covering my mouth with his, he let go. His dick seemed
to double in size, but I didn't care—it could have been
three, four times as big, and I'd have still wanted it.
I wanted him to keep fucking me, to stay inside until

he was ready to go again, to keep me pinned to that bench despite the growing awareness of the wooden slats digging into my back, the awkward angle of my neck, the pain in my legs, held up for so long.

But all good things must come to an end. Carefully holding the condom in place, he pulled out of me; I half expected my intestines, perhaps even my head, to follow through in the vacuum he left.

He sat beside me, breathing heavily, one hand on my aching thigh. I rested my head on his chest, and we kissed a little more.

"Come on," he said. "Shower."

"Yeah." We were lucky not to have been busted. One more kiss and we were out there, soaping up under the water like any other two guys at the gym.

He looked stunned when I asked his name and baffled when I suggested we go for a coffee; I guess most of his tricks didn't stick around. Maybe I wouldn't have if I hadn't found out that he was a lawyer. His huge dick wasn't the only attraction.

So we sat on a bench in Central Park, watching the ducks on Harlem Meer and sipping a couple of Starbucks coffees. It was a pleasant afternoon—but, more importantly, nobody could hear us talk in the park.

After the preliminaries (Martin Kingston, 56 years old, separated from his wife, grown-up kids), I got straight down to business.

"Have you heard of a company called Marshall Land?"

He sipped his coffee, wiped his beard and nodded. "Of course."

"Know much about them?"

"They're one of the more successful property developers in the greater New York area. Why?"

"Does the name Trey Peters mean anything to you?"

"Ah." He sipped his coffee again while a woman pushed her baby stroller past our bench. "Trey Peters."

"You've heard of him."

"Oh, yes." Sip, wipe. "The late Mr. Peters."

"And?"

"I believe there is a criminal investigation underway."

He wasn't this discreet when he was ramming his dick up my ass in the steam room. "Anyone who reads the papers knows that. I was kind of hoping you might know the inside story."

"Are you working for Marshall Land, Dan?" He half rose. "Because if you are, I must warn you…"

"Hey, calm down." I put a hand on his arm. "I'm not working for anybody. All I know is that somebody tried to kill me, and from what I can make out, that person was Julian Marshall."

He looked into my eyes—the same penetrating gaze I'd seen back at the gym—and said, "Go on."

So I told him everything, from my first visit from Enrico Ferrari right up to Jody's disappearance in Buffalo. I left nothing out—the unanswered call, the strange encounter with the cops, Jody's inexplicable mood swings, the too-convenient old couple in the adjacent room at the Starlight. Martin listened quietly, nodding his head and occasionally asking me to clarify a point.

"And the only thing I could think to do was to come back to New York and confront them," I said. "And then I met you." And you fucked some common sense into me, I should have added. You made me realize that I couldn't do this on my own. That even I, with my famous twelve years of combat experience, couldn't take on an organized crime outfit like Marshall's single-handed. I needed help, I needed to start working with the authorities, and I needed to ditch my action-hero fantasies.

"You never considered putting it in the hands of the police."

"I considered it."

"But you don't trust them?"

I shrugged.

"Okay, Dan. As it happens, I do know a couple of people involved in the Peters investigation."

"That's convenient."

"Just goes to show," said Martin, draining his coffee and lobbing the cup into the trash, "that you never know who you might pick up in a gym. What do you say we go back to my apartment and do a bit of planning. I'm just over at Morningside Heights."

"My place is closer." I nodded toward 109th Street.

"I'm sure it is. But Ferrari knows your address. Call me old-fashioned, but I really don't want anyone putting a bullet through your brain just yet." He put a hand on my leg and squeezed. "I've got other things in mind."

I followed him back to Morningside Heights like an eager puppy dog. It's great being an officer in the USMC, it's great fucking the asses of guys in their teens and twenties, but sometimes my heart belongs to daddy.

After a full night on the end of Martin Kingston's cock I was barely capable of walking, let alone figuring out how to bring down an organized crime ring. Fortunately, testing the limits of my ass seemed to help Martin to think clearly. He was up at seven o'clock, making coffee and phone calls, while I stumbled around the bathroom and washed the dried cum off my belly. When I emerged in nothing but a white towel, Martin was dressed in a shirt and tie.

"Breakfast?"

"Sure."

He put toast and cereal in front of me, while jabbing buttons on his phone.

"Jack? It's Martin. Hey, good, thanks." I ate while he talked; I was starving. "Listen, you're working on the Trey Peters case, right? Okay. Well, yeah, maybe. How does attempted murder and kidnapping sound? Pretty sure, yes." Martin stood behind me and rubbed my neck. "I've got a man here who has a tale to tell. You want to hear it?"

An hour later we were sitting in the lobby of a law firm on the corner of Broad and Wall Street. The floor was marble and the walls were made of some fancy yellow stone I don't even know the name of. Martin looked comfortable, his legs crossed, glancing at the front of the *New York Times*. I felt like a fish out of water, even in a borrowed shirt and pants. Anyone who noticed me sitting nervously on that leather sofa would have thought "criminal."

"Jack" turned out to be John Everett Rendell of Parker-Rendell, one of the best law firms in the city, as Martin told me as we rode the elevator to the eighteenth floor. I could believe it. This was the first time I've ever seen a potted palm actually inside an elevator.

"Martin!"

"Jack!"

There was a lot of handshaking and backslapping; Jack Rendell was maybe five years younger than Martin, and in excellent shape. I felt haggard and sleazy.

"This is Major Dan Stagg."

"Pleased to meet you, Major." Rendell had the firm handshake and intense gaze that I'd encountered in a few senior officers when I was a young marine. I stood a little taller. "Once a marine, always a marine, right?"

"Excuse me?"

"Self-defense training. The New Hampshire cops say you nearly killed that guy who broke into your room."

"Oh." I suppose I was glad to hear that he was alive, although one death more or less on my conscience doesn't make too much difference. "Should I write to say sorry?"

Rendell smiled. "Martin says you have something to tell me."

"Yeah, about…"

Before I could say more I was ushered into his office—I say "office," but it was more like a carpeted football field—and the door was closed behind us. One wall was entirely glass.

"Sit down. Coffee?"

"Sure."

He poured from a steel jug. "Relax, Major. We won't be disturbed."

Martin settled himself on an expensive contraption of brown leather and tubular steel, while Jack Rendell sat on his desk. On a low chair, I was at a distinct disadvantage. I recognized the technique. I've used it myself often enough. Always remind them who's boss. Hell, with the state my ass was in I hardly needed reminding. I was just grateful for the cushions.

We started at the beginning yet again—Enrico Ferrari's first visit to 109th Street, the safe-deposit box with its deadly contents, the delivery of Stirling McMahon at Penn Station.

"Do you by any chance still have the letter that Ferrari gave you?"

"I guess it's back at my apartment."

Rendell took a note. "And you'd be able to identify him, would you?"

"Sure." I thought of that handsome, movie-star mug. "He kind of stands out."

"Indeed." Rendell rubbed his chin; I wondered if he, like Martin, fucked men in steam rooms. "And this Stirling McMahon…"

"That's not his real name."

"Correct." He consulted a piece of paper. "Which one did he give you?"

"Jody Miller." Rendell nodded slowly. "Although it's really Muller."

He consulted a piece of paper. "Well, he's used Miller before. Now let me see. Jody." He scanned a list. "Hmm. No. That appears to be a new one." He made another note. "Go on."

"Wait a minute. You mean…"

"Your Jody Miller has been known by quite a number of aliases. Stirling McMahon, or sometimes McMasters, was his—what shall we say?—business name."

"As a hustler, right?"

"Indeed. And on a couple of adult websites."

"Oh." I felt sick. This was the guy I thought I was in love with. A hooker and a porn "star."

I still think it's better than killing people for a living…

"As far as we know, his real name is Brian Cooper."

"Where's he from?"

"His first criminal record is from Michigan."

"Well, that was true, at least." I carried on with the story—our road trip, the daily check-ins, the encounter with the police in New Hampshire.

"Can I just stop you for a moment?" Rendell flicked through some notes. "Could you give me an accurate date for that?"

I worked it out. Rendell nodded.

"That was the day after Cooper was meant to be interviewed by the NYPD in connection with the Trey Peters case."

"Is that why the New Hampshire cops were looking for him?"

"Yes. He was reported as a missing person, wanted in connection with a serious criminal investigation. A photograph had been sent out. Usual procedure."

"Shit." It's a fool who can't distinguish between friend and foe. I thought the New Hampshire police were in Marshall's pay. "Why didn't they just pick him up?"

"You tell me." Rendell put a photograph in my hands—a young man with short dark hair, staring vacantly into the camera. Even I, who had been fucking and kissing that face for a week, had to look twice to recognize Jody. "This was taken from a gay dating site on which Cooper was advertising his services as a masseur."

"He told me he'd taken his profiles down."

"He had. But these things never really go away. Has he changed much?"

"Yeah. He's blond now. Longer hair."

Rendell looked over at Martin and caught his eye. They both nodded slightly. "And does it suit him?"

"I guess," I said. "But I'd prefer him the way nature intended." There was one detail of the story that I hadn't yet told Rendell, although he'd have to be stupid not to figure it out.

"I take it that you and Mr. Cooper were..." He held his hand out, waggled it from side to side.

"Dan said he was the best piece of ass in the eastern United States," said Martin. "Although I'd have to question that."

Rendell laughed, and for a moment I wondered if

the Financial District was going to get a window view of Major Dan Stagg being double-fucked on the Parker-Rendell carpet.

"When Cooper was picked up in Buffalo," asked Rendell, "did he struggle?"

"Yeah." I tried to remember the scene. "A bit."

"A bit." Rendell nodded. "I see."

"You think it was a setup?"

"I don't rule out the possibility."

"How will we find out?"

"The police are treating it as abduction. That's all you need to know."

"Yeah, but one hustler more or less..."

"One hustler who may just enable us to break one of the nastiest criminal networks in New York City," said Rendell. "Besides, what's wrong with hustlers?"

Jack Rendell spent the rest of the day in briefings with officers from the NYPD. Martin escorted me to 109th Street, where I picked up anything I thought would be of interest to the investigation while the cab waited outside. Half an hour later I was back in Morningside Heights with a library of books and DVDs to occupy me, and a warning from Martin to keep indoors. "They may not know you're back in the city," he said, "but don't take any chances. What you just told Jack could put Julian Marshall in prison for a long time."

"Don't worry about me," I said. "I can take care of myself."

Another of those movie moments, right? Some niggling strings on the soundtrack, maybe, just so there's no doubt about what's coming. A quick montage of me sitting in Martin's apartment trying to read a book, trying to watch a movie, getting bored, raiding the fridge, pacing up and down, and eventually saying to myself, "Hell, I need some fresh air... What could possibly happen?" and taking the elevator down to the street. And then it'd be me walking along Riverside Drive, a tracking shot from inside a car. There'd be a pair of gloved hands on the steering wheel, a dirty windshield... Those niggling strings are back, more forceful this time; the audience shouts, "Dan! Look out! He's behind you!" but it's too late. The strings are drowned by the shriek of tires as the car mounts the sidewalk at full speed, hits my left knee with its right front fender, and down I go, only avoiding further damage by rolling away from the curb where the car can't get me. They peel off down the street, leaving me lying on the ground clutching my leg. It feels like it's broken.

In fact, as I found out in the emergency room, it wasn't even fractured. The joint swelled up like a melon and it hurt like fuck, but, as the doctor said, I'd live. They're all heart, those New York doctors. "The nurse will put a tube bandage on it," he said, and rushed on to the next cubicle.

"Gee, thanks, Doc," I muttered, but my mood improved when the curtain swished aside and a handsome young male nurse appeared at my bedside. It crossed my mind that the situation had potential, and given my tendency to indulge in recreational sex at critical moments I could easily have explored a few medical fantasies. For once, though, I thought, "Wait a minute, Dan. Martin will be worried about you. Jack Rendell, a partner in one of the city's biggest law firms, will be worried about you. In fact, the NYPD is probably looking for you." And so I limited myself to a smile and some unnecessary eye contact and didn't even ask the nurse what time he got off.

I took a cab back to Martin's apartment. He wasn't home. So much for the whole of Manhattan being in uproar; I hadn't been missed. I could have fucked that nurse...

I heard Martin's key in the lock five minutes later.

"Hey." He kissed me and took off his tie. I felt like I should produce a shaker of martinis and put a casserole on the table. "I'm exhausted."

"You should take a shower."

"Later. First of all I need to tell you something."

Me, too, I thought, but it would keep. "I'm listening."

"I met Julian Marshall this afternoon."

"Nice for you."

"It was surprisingly easy. I put on a southern accent and said I was a church minister who wanted to sell a large tract of land in Virginia." He sat down, legs apart. "They couldn't get me into that office fast enough."

"Very clever."

"And guess what I found out?"

"No idea."

He grabbed my leg—I nearly yelped with pain—and said, "Marshall's about to take an extended vacation. He said he'd like to send one of his representatives to survey the property, since he and his wife are planning a trip to Europe."

"Big place, Europe."

"So I gave him a few details, and I named a price

that was so low, I could practically see the dollar signs ringing up in his eyes, and said that we'd love for him to come visit with us next week. He offered me his associate, but I said we'd really set our hearts on dealing with Mr. Marshall himself because of his reputation as an upright citizen and a generous benefactor to the church. No, I couldn't possibly deal with his subordinates; it was Christ's work that I was on, and I kind of let him believe that I was doing some kind of shady deal behind the backs of the believers. Oh, he was squirming by this time, because nothing turns a man like Marshall on as much as stealing bread from the mouths of widders and orphans."

"That's not what Jody told me."

"We didn't get around to discussing that kind of thing." His hand rested on my thigh. "Anyway, I heard enough. He's frightened."

"I could have told you that. One of his goons tried to kill me this afternoon."

"What? Someone's been here?"

I confessed my little afternoon stroll and what came of it. He had my pants off within moments. "Jesus, Dan, what the hell did you think you were doing?"

I shrugged. "Getting some fresh air."

"These aren't some little local thugs we're dealing with here. This is serious stuff, boy."

"From what I can see they're amateurs. They've made three murder attempts so far, and they've all failed."

"They were warnings. You think they couldn't have killed you and Jody if they wanted to? Jesus, Dan, nothing's easier."

Was he right? Did the guy in the Starlight Motel let

me disarm him on purpose? And what about Jody's encounter with a gun on 54th Street? Had that even happened?

"Point taken. What next?"

"We've made our move, they've made theirs. They may not yet know that we've seen Jack Rendell, but they'll soon find out. They know you're in the City, and they know where you're staying. Marshall's ready to skip town, because he knows the net is closing. It's a question of who moves first—the cops or Marshall. All we can do now is wait."

And so we waited. We stayed in Martin's apartment, only venturing as far as the shop on the corner for food. He wouldn't let me out on my own, and he wouldn't leave me in the apartment. If it wasn't for that little hit-and-run, I'd think he was the possessive type. We talked over and over what had happened, trying to figure out if anything Jody told me was true, wondering whether my little "accident" on Riverside Drive was a warning or more, anticipating Marshall's next move. Occasionally the phone rang—Jack Rendell or his associates reporting on the investigation into the Trey Peters case, digging up some interesting facts on Marshall Land and their shady employee, Enrico Ferrari. When Martin told Rendell about Marshall's vacation plans, all hell broke loose. And everyone said the same thing: *Stay where you are. Don't answer the door. Don't leave the building. Report anything suspicious.*

When we were all talked out, we took a shower and spent a while in bed, and I must say there's some truth in the old belief that pain in one part of the body distracts you from pain elsewhere, because after Martin had fucked me again, my bruised, swollen knee felt a hell of a lot better.

We slept and ate and fooled around a bit more, and in between times Martin took phone calls.

By evening we had learned two very important things. First, there was a pretrial hearing in three days at which a judge would consider the evidence against Julian Marshall and his associates in connection with the death of Trey Peters. If the evidence was insufficient, it was unlikely that the case would ever come to court. Secondly, Marshall Land was about to finalize a deal transferring substantial holdings to a company in Liberia.

"Why don't they just arrest him?"

Martin stroked my chest; we were lying naked on the couch. "Because they don't have enough evidence to charge him yet."

"They'd arrest him if he was some bum on the street."

"Correct. Welcome to my world, Dan."

I hope I'm painting a cozy picture: me and my new Daddy in a smart apartment in Morningside Heights, playing with each other while the cops and lawyers do the real work. And that's how it should have stayed— but the enemy was a little smarter, or more desperate, than we had calculated.

The phone rang at precisely nine o'clock, at which time Martin was sitting back on the sofa wearing a white terrycloth dressing gown, his legs wide apart and me kneeling between them, making up for lost time. Though I'm usually the commanding officer in such scenes, I liked being Daddy's boy for a change. The phone rang as I was enjoying the challenge of attempting to get both Martin's balls in my mouth, and he was rubbing my bald head in encouragement.

"Martin...nnnnghff!...Kingston, hello? Hi, yes..."

And then he froze, one ball in my mouth.

"Oh, Jesus. Linda? Hello? Linda? What? Who the fuck is this? What have you done to my little girl?"

I jumped to my feet and pulled on some clothes. Martin's face was as white as a sheet, and he was gesturing frantically for paper and pen. He scribbled some details—an address, a time, NO POLICE underlined three times.

"Hello? Hello?"

He put the phone down. His face was white, and he looked very old.

"They've got my daughter."

I sat beside him, put an arm around his shoulder. "Don't worry. We'll get her back. I'm trained for this kind of thing."

"If I bring anyone with me, they will kill her."

"What?"

He told me everything—the rendezvous arrangements, the ransom, the usual conditions: come alone, no police, no publicity. The grisly details of what they would do to Linda if Martin disobeyed. There was no doubt in either of our minds who "they" were. We didn't even ask each other. Martin had been to see Marshall, I'd been seen at Martin's address, they almost certainly knew that we'd been talking to Jack Rendell. The heat was on, the deadline approaching, and they were getting dangerous. They struck where they knew we were vulnerable, dividing the opposition with one ruthless stroke. It was tactically admirable. Martin was already dressing, his mind focused on one thing only. When he looked at me he scowled—of course, all this was my fault. One steam room fuck and now his daughter's life was at risk.

"Martin, I've got to come with you."

"You stay right here." His voice was loud and harsh, and from the look on his face I knew better than to argue.

"At least let me call the cops."

"No. Don't you dare screw this up."

"But they're..."

"No!" Jesus—he reminded me of a bullying sergeant I'd known in my junior days. He made an effort to calm down. "I've got to do this myself. Stay here and don't do anything."

No point in arguing. He was out the door. But what was I supposed to do now? Sit tight like a good little boy and wait for the nasty men to go away? Oh, sure. Just my style. No—the moment Martin left I was figuring out my strategy. "No cops," they said. Okay. No cops. But I still have guns, and if I can't outmaneuver a bunch of gangsters like Marshall and Ferrari, then I'll send my medals back to Uncle Sam, postpaid.

You don't rush these things. You sit down and think, with a cool and logical head. So twenty minutes later I was at Martin's desk, making a list. The two Glock 19s were loaded and ready in my knapsack on the table.

And that's when the doorbell rang.

Martin lives in one of those fancy apartments with a video-entry phone at street level, intercoms on every floor, controlled access to every landing—your typical paranoid New Yorker's domestic fortress, basically. The final frontier is a bell on the apartment door which sets off a discreet, muffled ding-dong that won't disrupt the flow of your discreet dinner party. In theory, the only people who could ring your bell without first going through every other level of security were your next-door neighbors.

"Who is it?"

"Martin? It's Jerry."

"Jerry?"

"Jerry from apartment five, man."

Yeah, right. I walked toward the table where my knapsack lay, Glock inside, saying, "Sorry, man, Martin's not here. I'll tell him you came by."

No need – next thing I knew the lock had been shot open by a Glock with a silencer, and I was shoved up against the wall. It was not Jerry from apartment five.

"Hello, Dan."

"Hello, Ferrari." There were three of them. "Who are your friends?"

I put up a decent fight and got within an inch or two of pushing them out, but three against one is bad odds. I ended up winded, sprawling on the floor.

"Nice of you to visit," I said, picking myself up. Ferrari was pointing a gun at my head.

"Make a noise, faggot, and see what happens." He clicked his fingers, and one of the goons grabbed my wrists while the other secured them behind my back with cable ties. "Search the place."

It didn't take them long to find the guns.

"Planning a little exercise, Dan?" Ferrari calmly

unloaded the weapons and handed them to his associate, who put them neatly away in an attaché case.
Out on the street the three of them would pass for busi-
nessmen—charcoal suits, white shirts, dark ties. Busi-
nessmen or upscale gangsters—it's so hard to tell the
difference these days.

"Get down on your knees."

I did as I was told—not because after a couple of
days with Martin Kingston's cock stretching my ass I'd
turned into an obedient sub, but because Ferrari had
taken the safety off and looked as if he might decide on
a swift execution if I didn't follow orders. He stood in
front of me, cool as a fucking cucumber. Marshall Land's
business methods were brutal, but obviously effective. I
wondered how many more Trey Peterses there had been
over the years? How many more secretaries silenced?
How many witnesses taken out of state?

"Boss getting jumpy, Ferrari?" My eyes were at
crotch level. "Send you to clean up his mess again?"

"Shut up, Dan." He didn't sound angry—more like a
tired father telling off an annoying four year old.

"Where's Jody?"

"Who?"

"Stirling. Marshall's boyfriend."

"Oh, him." He smiled, as if he'd remembered something funny. "You don't have to worry about Stirling
anymore. We're taking good care of him."

I tried to sound cool. "Have you killed him?"

"What? Dan, really, you surprise me. Of course we
haven't killed him. We like to look after our employees—
especially when they've done a good job. We like to
reward them."

So Jody was lying all along? His kidnapping was a setup? Ferrari saw the confusion on my face, and laughed. "Sorry to burst your bubble, asshole. Hey!" He clicked his fingers. "One of you meatheads shut this freak up for me."

I braced myself for the blow, expecting the butt of a gun to the back of my head. But no—one of them held me in a stranglehold while the other prepared a hypodermic needle.

"Just a little prick, Dan," said Ferrari, laughing and scratching his balls. "Goodnight, asshole."

I felt the scratch in the crook of my elbow, felt a nauseating heat rushing up my arm to my heart, and then someone switched off the lights.

The Room 10

I was lying on my back and I was cold. My hands and feet were secured to—what? A bed frame? Felt like metal. My arms were away from my body, my legs spread. Underneath me was a blanket or thin mattress. Apart from the straps at my wrists and ankles, I was naked.

I ran a mental checklist. It's basic training; you assess your injuries in order to evaluate your chances of escape. Starting at the top: no major pain in the head. I ran my tongue over my teeth: all present and correct. No cuts to the lips, and the jaw was mobile. No obvious injury to the torso and arms, and when I wiggled my fingers they seemed to work. Clenching my thigh muscles I worked down my legs: everything where it should be, right to the tips of my toes.

I couldn't yet remember what happened and how I got here. You don't waste your effort on memory; you think about now and the next five minutes. Am I injured? Is my life in immediate danger? Survival first.

Basic checks done, I turned my attention to the

outside world—which, at the moment, was reduced to a single brightly-lit circle in which hovered a face. It took a few moments before the dazzle and the jumble of features arranged themselves into something recognizable.

Enrico Ferrari.

"Stagg."

His voice sounded flat and distant, like next door's TV. The whole scene had an air of unreality, something viewed down the wrong end of a telescope. Far, far away was a naked man strapped to a metal bed frame, another man bending over him...

"Wake up, Stagg."

The voice and picture were getting closer, and I felt myself coming in to land.

Ouch. The ties at my wrists and ankles were digging into the flesh and they fucking hurt. My back ached; how long had I been out? And I was cold—freezing cold. I started to shiver, the body's first instinctive attempt to warm itself. That stopped me from speaking for a while. I screwed up my eyes, and when I opened them again Ferrari was gone. Just a circle of bright white light and the faint ghost of an image where his face had been, strange purples and greens hovering around my retina. Eyes. Noses. Mouths.

"Hey!"

My voice sounded ridiculously loud in my head. No echo. A small room, then, furnished or at least carpeted.

I was still shivering, and from the pain in my throat when I spoke I figured that I had a fever of some sort. Maybe just the drugs wearing off... That's right. I remember the sting of the needle as it punctured my skin, the dizzying descent into unconsciousness. Ferrari arriving at the apartment... Whose apartment? I couldn't quite recall. Someone I had lost... Martin, that's right. He'd gone... Why...

"Daughter."

My voice again, although this time I wasn't aware I'd spoken. Jesus, whatever they'd given me was some strong shit. Daughter...of course, Martin's daughter. Kidnapped. Rendezvous, ransom, "no cops," Jerry from apartment number five, and here I was.

"You bastard, Ferrari."

Soft voices somewhere in the room. Two? Three? Not more. I tried to lift my head to look around. A bolt of pain shot through my skull, and I had to swallow hard in order not to vomit. It's not good to vomit when you're lying on your back. People die.

Okay, Dan. Deep breaths. You're not injured. Maybe you're sick; maybe it's just the stuff they shot you up with. Wait until the pain passes. Don't throw up. You're too weak to do anything. Try to remember. Gather information.

There was something hovering around the edge of my consciousness. Something bad and weird and sad. What had Ferrari told me? Just before I went out. Something...someone... A face I couldn't focus on, a name I couldn't remember...

Stirling. Stirling or...what was the other name? I went through a list. Will? Kenny? Martin? Scott? See, I could remember some cheap city slicker who gave me forty bucks for the fuck of his life but I couldn't recall the name of the guy who, just a couple of days ago, I was supposed to be in love with.

Jody. That's it. Jody. Or possibly Brian. I smiled with relief. I wasn't losing my mind after all.

But there was still something wrong. Something Ferrari said...

We like to look after our employees—especially when they've done a good job. We like to reward them...

A good job.

What?

What had Jody done? What had he achieved, apart from leading me on a pointless journey across New England? What obscure purpose was behind it? Why had I allowed myself to become involved, to fall in love? Whose game was this? Julian Marshall? Enrico Ferrari? Trey Peters? I didn't know who to trust. Martin Kingston? Jack Rendell? Were they all in on this—whatever this was?

"Will."

I said that word out loud, good and clear. It sounded firm and solid, something to hold on to.

"What?"

Ferrari's face again, hovering in the circle of blinding light. Black eyebrows, slits for eyes, a mask. The features flew around, arranging themselves in crazy new patterns, and I sank down into the blackness.

What happened next could have been a dream—my dreams can be really vivid. I saw Jody Miller straddling my cock, as he had so many times before in motel rooms and rental cars, riding up and down, reaching around behind to stretch his ass around me, the other hand rubbing up and down his firm stomach.

I was sure it was Jody. It felt like Jody. I tried to see his face, but there was too much light behind him, too much swirling darkness. I felt the sensation in my dick, the pressure in my balls, and then I lost him; the picture spun off into space and I slept again.

The next time I came around I was aware of two things. I was in pain—felt like I had a broken rib on my left side, and my head was throbbing from the crown right down to the jaw, as if someone had slapped or punched me repeatedly. And I was alone. I don't know how I figured that out—it was a feeling that became a certainty. I struggled to look around—nothing. I held my breath and listened—nothing, not even the sound of someone else breathing. I was still cold, but something had been thrown over me—a sheet or blanket. I moved a bit and felt rough cloth on my naked body. I twisted my left hand a little—the sheet stuck. Dried blood is like glue if you leave it long enough.

What had happened? How long had I been here? I'd been heavily sedated, that was for sure—and beaten up while I was unconscious. Seems weird. Why anesthetize someone if you want to cause them pain? Why kidnap someone unless you're going to interrogate them? Why kidnap me at all? I was no use to anybody. No one was going to pay a ransom to get me released. I didn't know anything. I was hired muscle when that was needed, a driver and a bodyguard who'd been pushed around like a piece on a chessboard and now... What? Kill me—yeah, that I could understand. I'd talked to lawyers and policemen, I'd threatened the Marshall Land sell-out and possibly sabotaged Julian Marshall's vacation plans. But why go to the trouble of holding me in this little dungeon or office or whatever the hell it was? Why waste good sedatives on me? That stuff has a street value. You don't just stick it in any old vein.

Someone was coming; I heard footsteps on a hard floor, getting closer, then stopping. The soft whoosh of the door being opened, a change of acoustics, and the sound of breathing. I kept my eyes almost closed—open just enough to register movement in the room.

"Stagg?"

Ferrari's voice, or one like it. I was getting kind of used to it.

"Stagg?"

He spoke quietly, perhaps not wanting anyone else to hear—perhaps not really wanting to wake me. I said nothing, didn't move.

The door closed. I strained my ears. Was I alone? The faintest click—the sound of someone opening their mouth. He was here. He was close.

"Dan Stagg." The voice was soft, the tone appraising. "So that's what all the fuss is about." I felt cool air on my chest and stomach; the sheet was being lifted, pulled back. I didn't move, kept my breathing regular and my eyes closed. "A dirty old man."

You can talk, I thought—I bet you've traded your ass for a position at Marshall Land. Why else would Julian Marshall employ such a pretty boy as his lieutenant? What's behind the sharp suits, the precise grooming, the carefully structured mask of machismo? Sorry, buster, but when it comes to sniffing out a closet case, you set a thief to catch a thief.

The sheet was down to my hips now, and despite the pain and the bruising I felt my torso tingling, the hair on my chest standing up, my nipples hardening. Did Ferrari notice? Did he have an eye for these details? It seemed he did. Something brushed over my left tit—something light, the back of his hand perhaps. Not quite touching my skin, just stroking the hair. Come on, scared boy. Take what you want. Then maybe we can talk.

Was this the drugs talking? Was I still half-crazy—imagining that the man who had kidnapped and half-killed me was now about to fuck me? Was this the onset of Stockholm syndrome? For all I knew he was preparing to administer another injection, or scoping out the target for a knife or a bullet. Just by the heart, into the lungs, that would do the job. A vacant bed, and another body to dispose of.

"Fucking queers."

His voice was low, almost rasping. It was not the voice of an efficient, cold-blooded killer. On the other hand it could easily be the voice of a psychopath who's working himself up to a bloodbath.

"Hey, Jackson!"

Loud this time—so loud I almost flinched. The sheet went back over my body. Footsteps from somewhere, a distant voice. "Yes, boss?"

"How long ago did we give this one his dope?"

"Four hours." The door opened, and the voice—Jackson—was in the room.

"When will he come around?"

"Hour or two."

"Where's Gambino?"

"He's making the delivery, like you told him. Left about forty-five minutes ago."

"That's all. Get lost, Jackson. Go take out the trash."

"Okay, boss." Door closed, footsteps receding, alone

again with Enrico Ferrari and his wandering hands.

The delivery...take out the trash...Jackson and Gambino, the two goons. Nobody else was mentioned. What—or who—was being delivered? What—or who— was the trash? Was Jody here? Was it just a dream? Whose side was he on? Was he hurt? Dead? My heart thumped.

Ferrari was breathing harder. I opened my eyes enough to see him pacing up and down the room—five paces away, five paces back. Five away, five back. He had the air of a man making up his mind about something.

Hour or two...

He thought I was still well and truly sedated. He'd dismissed his subordinates. We were alone in a closed room, no witnesses, and he was stressing about something. I could only think of two things: sex, or murder.

Given that my arms and legs were still secured, I really hoped it was the former.

The pacing stopped. Whatever was going to happen was going to happen soon. He was breathing like a man who's spent ten minutes on the treadmill. All my senses were telling me that this was a man with sex on his mind. Touch—those fingers brushing my chest. Smell—the smoky smell of a hot man. Sight—his restless pacing. Sound—the heavy breathing. All that was left was taste, and that wasn't far behind.

He unzipped his fly, half-mounted the bed, and rubbed the head of his cock against my lips. It was wet and sticky and salty. Yeah, I know that taste, Ferrari. So you get off on raping unconscious men, do you? A little bit of necrophilia. That how you square it with your macho Mafia facade? Okay. Not my idea of fun—I like 'em wide awake and most definitely alive—but there was potential here. Not the kind of potential I'm usually thinking of—but the possibility of escape.

It didn't look good: I was drugged and bound, he was almost certainly armed. But the fact that he was rubbing his stiff cock against my unresisting lips was the first hopeful signal I'd had in a while.

It felt good, and I would have been quite happy to suck it properly, but I reminded myself that I was supposed to be out cold. So I let him smoosh his sticky cockhead around my mouth and chin until it was coated with sticky stuff. Jesus, I thought, he must be very horny if he's leaking like that. Poor bastard, hiding and pretending, and now that he's got what he wanted, all he can do is scratch his dickhead against my stubble.

"Fucking queer…" The voice even softer and rougher now, the sound of a man drifting into fantasy. Pathetic shithead, hating on the thing he really is. But there would be time for anger later. All I needed to know at this moment was that Ferrari's dick was getting harder, that his hand was stroking my face, grabbing my chin, and that he was climbing further on to the bed in an attempt to penetrate my mouth properly. I guess he was planning to straddle my chest and fuck my face. I remembered how good his thighs and ass looked in those tight grey pants, and my cock started to stir.

Unlikely, isn't it? My life's in danger, I've been beaten up, my ribs hurt so much with Ferrari clambering over me that it feels like someone's sticking a kitchen knife in my side—and I'm getting a hard-on. I registered the sensation with surprise. In a combat situation—which this was, despite the unorthodox position—your genitals usually shrivel. God's way of protecting them for the better times. So why was I getting so very stiff? How come my cock was lifting the sheet off my body? How long before Ferrari noticed? At the moment he was intent on my mouth, but all he had to do was reach behind him or look around and he was going to see that I wasn't as unconscious as I was meant to be.

It didn't take long. In clambering on to the bed Ferrari slid one leg over my body and encountered resistance. Several hard inches of resistance.

"What the fuck..." he breathed, and grabbed me through the cloth. "Jesus. My god." Like many men of his type, Ferrari turned to religion in times of temptation. He twisted around, the better to see what was in his hand. He squeezed, testing its girth. "How much did they give you?" he muttered. "Hey, Stagg!" A little louder. "Stagg!"

Making sure I was still unconscious? Hoping to wake me for playtime? Either way was dangerous. I hedged my bets and managed a groan, opening my mouth wide enough to let his cockhead in. One groan quickly became a duet. I made sure he didn't encounter teeth. Pushing his hips forward, Ferrari started to slip into my mouth—it was dry in there, I needed water, but he didn't seem to mind—holding on to my dick behind him like a cowboy on a bronco saddle. Okay, I thought, we're in business. One of us isn't thinking straight, and it ain't the one with a head full of anesthetic and a dick full of Viagra, or whatever they'd given me. How can I turn this situation around? I'm bound hand and foot to a metal bedstead, I'm sucking a man who probably has a gun, and if I do something stupid, like biting him, he'll probably kill me. He's so hopped up on self-hatred he could do anything. I really don't want to die because of Enrico Ferrari's fucked-up libido.

I opened up a little wider and brought my tongue into play, letting it move around the underside of his head, feeling the taut string of skin leading down from his pisshole. That did the trick—my salivary glands woke up and gave me enough spit to turn this from a dry, forced entry into something more like a blow job. Ferrari noticed the difference and let out a sigh. His left hand cupped the back of my head—fuck, that hurt; someone had hit me there and someone was going to pay—and his right hand plucked at the sheet, pulling it off my lower half. I felt the air on my stiff cock before Ferrari grabbed it again.

"Fucking big dick," he said. "Think you're the man, don't you, Stagg? The fucking marine major. Well look at you now. You fucking pussy."

Good. Keep it coming, asshole. While you're going into meltdown, I'm figuring out just what it would take to turn this creaking metal frame upside down and pin you underneath it. It's already top heavy. If I could just raise my knees enough to swing them violently to one side the whole thing might tilt and topple, and you'd be the one on the ground fighting for breath...

"Cocksucker. Look at your mouth working on my dick. You fucking love it, don't you?"

Lines from a porn movie, no doubt, something he'd watched furtively on his PC. This was my cue. I groaned some more and opened my eyes a little, just enough for Ferrari to see that I was coming around. He stopped playing with my cock, like a kid caught with its hand in the cookie jar.

"You're awake."

My eyelids fluttered. It wasn't just acting; my eyeballs felt so fucking dry that the skin was sticking to them.

"How long you been awake, faggot?"

Long enough to figure out your little game, Ferrari. "Hunhnhnh?" I couldn't say much more with his cock in my mouth. He seemed to realize that this was a bit of a giveaway and sprang smartly off the bed. Fuck! The pain in my ribs shot through me, and I felt sick.

"Where..."

"Don't ask questions." He quickly replaced the sheet. My dick had gone down a bit from the agony of cracked ribs. "Listen to me, Stagg, and listen good." More movie lines, this time some cheesy gangster flick. Everything about Ferrari was fake, from his expensive tailoring to his tough-guy attitude.

I tried to look scared. That seemed to work.

"You're going to die today. I can make it fast, or I can make it slow."

"Jody..."

He sneered. "Don't worry about your little friend. We've taken care of him."

"I thought..." Jesus, my throat hurt, like someone stuck a toilet brush down there. "Thought he was working for you."

"So did he, the sucker." Ferrari laughed. "Hey, that's not bad. Sucker. That's what he is, right? A cock-sucker. Like you, Stagg. Like the rest of them. All cock-suckers."

So did he... What did he mean? Had Jody been in

on the plot—whatever the hell the plot was? *We like to look after employees...reward them for a job well done.* How much had Jody known when we were on the road? He lied about everything, including his name, over and over. Why should I believe any of the bullshit about Trey Peters and the wire and the intended drug overdose? It was all lies, the sob story about his childhood, the innocent-little-hooker act, the roadside abduction... And then I remembered something from a dream—Jody Miller riding my cock. Not in some motel room, or the driver's seat of a car, but here, on this bed, with my arms and legs tied. What the fuck was going on? What was real, what was hallucination? Was I dreaming all this now? I pulled my arms out from the metal bedframe and felt the cable ties digging into my flesh. That pain was real, all right. I was awake. This was no dream, no more than Ferrari straddling my chest was a dream. The situation was complicated, for sure, but there are few situations that can't be improved with a bit of brute force. Just a question of getting the enemy off his guard and waiting for your opportunity.

I waited.

And while I waited, I discovered that the tie on my right wrist—the side away from where Ferrari now stood—was not as tight as it might have been. There was, perhaps, half an inch of play. Jackson or Gambino or whoever fixed me to the bed had been in too much of a hurry. Maybe it was Ferrari himself, nervous when it came to manhandling a naked man. Scared of giving himself away.

Okay, Ferrari, have your fun, because that half inch of play is going to be the death of you. Slowly, methodically, blocking out the pain, I rotated my wrist, scraping the radius against the plastic band until the skin was broken and bleeding. But with each turn the cable got a little looser.

Ferrari had stuffed his dick back into his pants but had forgotten to do up his fly. It was easy to see that he was still aroused. That suited me. The more blood in his dick, the less in his brain.

"You won't get away with this," I whispered. I could speak in movie lines as well as anyone.

"Yeah, right." Ferrari's hand wandered back to his dick. "And who's going to come to the rescue? Nobody knows where the hell you are, Stagg, and nobody cares." He pulled his cock out again, too turned on to keep it where it belonged. "You've been here for two days. Little bit late for the cavalry." He started stroking himself with one hand, feeling my chest with the other. "You're going to die, Stagg."

He pinched my tit—hard, of course; he had to hurt me. I saw his tongue run over his lips. My dick was getting stiff again.

"You're going to suck this, aren't you?"

I opened my mouth and let my tongue rest on my lower lip.

"Yeah!" A note of triumph in his voice. "You're all the same. Just like your little friend. Right at the end he was begging for a dick up his ass." He twisted my tit; god, it hurt. "Your dick. Didn't know that, did you? You were fucking him just when we..." Thump! He rammed his fist into my stomach. "Decided..." Thump! Again, harder, but this time I tensed to resist, trying to block the stabbing pain. "To *kill him!*" Another blow in the gut, but this time with an open hand that rested on the hairy ridges of my abdomen, moving up and down, feeling the sweat and the muscles.

One hand on my stomach, the other hand on his dick.

Careless, Ferrari. Careless, you murdering bastard.

I kept working my wrist around and around, side to side, feeling the blood trickling over my skin. Soon it would be loose enough to tear my hand free—leaving half the flesh behind, perhaps, but that would heal. I'm not frightened of injuries. As Ferrari can see, looking all over my body like he is, I'm covered in scars.

He was good and hard. I knew how he felt. When you spend your life hiding the way you feel, then even the most degraded sexual encounter is enough to send your dick super-stiff. I guess Ferrari had been waiting a long time to get me alone. Well, now he was going to get what was coming to him. It wasn't quite what he expected—a rough blow job before he strangled me or shot me, silencing the only witness. The harder I could make him—the more I played along with his fantasy— the better my chances of escape.

His dick was back at my lips; he seemed to have a one-track mind. I licked him in welcome, and he shuddered. "Oh, fuck..." I placed my lips around his head and started moving up. The angle was painful in the extreme, but I figured if I could get him in a couple more inches—just as far as that midshaft point where his dick thickened like a zeppelin—then I'd have him at my mercy.

His left hand traveled down my stomach and under the sheet, where it found what it wanted. He grabbed my cock and started tugging. The other hand moved to my left bicep, squeezing it hard as Ferrari started to fuck my mouth. He was raised up on his tiptoes, and my head was skewed around in a position you only usually see on dead people. If this had been my first experience of sex, I don't think I'd have bothered coming back for more. Okay, I had a chemically-induced erection, and Ferrari's rough handling was sending some basic plea-sure signals to my brain—as was the taste and feel of his cock in my mouth—but the pain tipped the balance. My neck felt like it was breaking, that invisible kitchen knife was still plunging between my ribs, bloody chunks were coming off my bound wrist—and over all of this washed the sick dread that Jody really was dead.

Just when we decided to kill him.

It took all my training not to chomp down hard on Ferrari's prick and spit the fucking thing against the wall. But that would never happen. He'd shoot me the moment he felt my jaws tightening. Maybe I'd break the skin, cause him some pain and embarrassment in the emergency room—"You appear to have tooth marks around the base of your penis, Mr. Ferrari"—but I'd pay with my life.

Too high a price.

So I kept on sucking and working that wrist, and I breathed deeply through my nose, feeling his hand working on my cock, feeling the ache building in my balls. From the way Ferrari was panting and cursing, he wasn't far off either. He shuffled his pants down around his thighs—at least he had to stop squeezing my arm to do that—and half-climbed onto the bed. This enabled him to fuck me hard in the mouth—I was gagging, but he didn't care. He was in the final stages of the ride, and his concentration was shot. I was working that right wrist hard now, pretty certain that the gap was big enough. If I could free that hand then I'd push him over and twist us both to the floor...

"Oh, Jesus...Jesus..."

Was the angle right? Was I risking my one chance of escape on a bad calculation? His feet were still on the ground—he could brace quickly and stop me. If only he'd move his legs.

Ferrari was twisting around on top of me—I couldn't see what he was doing, but from the way the weight was shifting it felt like he was turning... Could it be? Toward my...

"Fuck!"

With one sudden move he swiveled around, pivoting on his dick which never left my lips, and lunged toward my groin. This, finally, was what he wanted. His mouth closed over my cock and his lips slid down. We were in a 69 position, Ferrari lying on top of me, and we were both starting to come. I tasted him in my mouth, felt my own cock throbbing in his, and just as I lost all my senses in the brutal mixture of pain and pleasure I tore my right hand free of its restraint and pushed as hard as I could against his hip. Precariously balanced as he was, his body already jerking in the throes of orgasm, he rolled straight over as I clung on to his waist. One agonizing shunt of my hips was enough; the bed, which was already creaking and complaining under the weight of two men, collapsed sideways to the ground. I managed to disengage my mouth during the fall; Ferrari was not so fortunate and landed on his back with me and the bed on top of him, the entire weight pushing through my cock and into his throat. I couldn't see him, but I could hear him—tearing gagging noises, and the feel of saliva flooding around my shaft. After fucking his mouth once, twice, three times for luck, until I was sure he was either unconscious or dead, I pulled out.

The commotion summoned Jackson, who burst through the door and took a couple of seconds to comprehend the scene before he drew his gun. He was fast, but I was faster. I'd already felt the weapon in Ferrari's waistband, and I didn't waste time in talking. Jackson took a bullet in the chest, the impact pushing him back out through the door.

If my luck held, then Gambino still hadn't come back from "making the delivery." I had a bad feeling about that delivery. Sounded all too likely to be a dead body, destination the bottom of the river.

It was just me, Ferrari and Jackson, both of them unconscious, both of them quite possibly dead. No— Ferrari was breathing after a fashion. It was ragged and noisy, and he may have sustained some damage to his windpipe if my dick went down the wrong way at the moment of impact, but he was alive. If he was lucky, I'd put him into the recovery position before I split. As for Jackson—well, I'd deal with him when I'd got myself free from the bed, to which I was still attached at three points. My right wrist was bleeding freely; I needed to staunch that pretty damn quick.

Ferrari had keys in his pocket. Keys, as everyone knows, are a reasonable substitute for a blade. I needed one with a toothed edge—something that, with a little application, would chew its way through a plastic cable tie. And so I sat on the floor, in a puddle of my own blood and what looked like Ferrari's vomit, and sawed through the ties, one after another. It took a little over ten minutes. Every so often I stopped to listen for cars or footsteps or voices. Nothing. No indication of where we were—the city, the country, up high, underground. There were no windows. We could have been anywhere.

Finally I was free: bleeding, bruised, broken and naked, but free. I rolled Ferrari and then Jackson onto their sides—no point in being unnecessarily cruel—and with torn strips of the filthy sheet I bound my bleeding wrist and even did something to stop the bleeding from Jackson's chest. He looked pale and sweaty. He might easily die. That was Gambino's problem.

And now, all I wanted to do was get out and get back to the City.

I needed clothes first. I ran down a long passage with bare concrete walls and a carpeted floor, a fluorescent tube flickering and buzzing at the far end. Double doors led through to what looked like an empty warehouse; it smelled faintly of gasoline, and more strongly of piss. I kept to the wall; here, at least, there was a cement path. The rest of the floor was covered in puddles and god knows what ankle-breaking obstacles. There were pigeons somewhere up in the roof; I could hear them calling and flapping. And it was cold as hell. I was glad to be moving, getting some warmth back into my body after the exposure and shock of the last few hours.

At the far end another door led into another passage, off which there were more doors—offices, I guess, from when this old place had been a going concern. Well, there might be something to clothe me in one of them, even if it was only a moldy old janitor's coat. I tried each door—locked, locked, locked. And the final one? Open an inch or two into deeper blackness within. I stopped and listened and sniffed. It smelled of shit. Damn it— some homeless guy, perhaps. I didn't much want to find out. I was about to turn away when my eyes, adjusting to the darkness, caught sight of something pale on the ground. White, and dirty. A glove, I thought at first. No. A hand, palm up, on the filthy floor.

I felt sick, and I was shaking as I pushed the door. It wouldn't move much, of course; the body was behind it. But I shifted it enough to slip inside and crouch down, and I knew, even in the near-darkness of that stinking room, that it was Jody.

The Sting **11**

Half an hour later, Jody was in an ambulance
speeding its way to the nearest emergency room—which
turned out to be in Trenton, New Jersey, another state
to add to my itinerary of the last week—and I was in
the back of a police car on the way to New York City
being debriefed over the telephone while a paramedic
attempted to strap up my chest and clean my wounds.

You can achieve a lot in half an hour if you put your
mind to it. I was naked, bleeding heavily and in a great
deal of pain from a broken rib; I'd also just discovered
Jody at death's door, which might have been harder to
deal with had I not encountered death so frequently in
my military career. However, getting help when you're
naked in enemy territory isn't that easy. I covered Jody
with some old plastic sheeting and ran out to the yard.
Tire tracks in the dirt led me to a twelve-foot-high gate
in the chain-link perimeter fence, topped off with razor
wire. I had no particular desire to lose my balls, and
unless I was very lucky no passing motorist was going to
stop for a crazy bleeding naked guy. I needed pants.

"Hey!"

A guy with a gun was running toward me. Most people would see that as a threat. I just saw it as a suit of clothes with an inconvenient body inside.

"Stop or I'll shoot!"

I stopped. There was nothing to fear. If he was worth anything as a guard he'd have shot on sight. Tut tut, Marshall, hiring amateurs. Bad move. I put my hands up.

"What the fuck you doing?" He approached me with caution, waving the gun. He was young and scrawny, midtwenties, I guess, a mean little gangster.

I did my best wild, confused stare, and even managed to dribble a bit. A drug-fucked loony. What possible harm could I do? I bent my legs, tensed the muscles.

"Fucking freak," he said, laughing through a nose that was soon going to be mashed into his ugly skull. "I'm going to kick your—"

I never found out which part of me he was intending to kick, because as soon as the gun was pointing away from my head I sprang, brought him down on his back and punched repeatedly into his face. Blood spurted out of his nostrils. I disarmed him and used the butt of the gun to knock him out—what we used to call a field anesthetic. Within five minutes I was fully dressed and climbing over the fence. I still looked pretty scary—black sweater, black boots, khaki combat pants, the usual pseudo-military shit—but at least you couldn't see my dick, and the only thing that got torn on the razor wire was the seat of my pants. The road was a quarter of a mile away, and it didn't take long to flag down a truck. Truck drivers, I guess, are less nervous than commuters hurrying home to their wives.

There was no time for pleasantries; I didn't even ask where the fuck I was.

"I need to call the cops. Right now."

He was the silent type—just dialed 911 and handed me his phone.

Like I said, one call was all it took. A few key words—among them "Julian Marshall"—and things happened fast. I left the driver to explain our where-abouts, checked that the guard was still unconscious and ran back to Jody. He was alive, but if an ambulance didn't get here pretty damn quick he might not last for long. I stripped off, lay down beside him and piled the clothes and plastic sheeting on top of us. The least I could do was warm him up. I held him gently and waited for the sirens. He was barely breathing when the ambulance arrived.

I didn't much care what happened to me. When the cops arrived I half expected them to arrest me for nearly killing the would-be assassin in the Starlight Motel. I was holding out my wrists for the cuffs. Instead, they treated me like a celebrity. Straight into the back of a cruiser, personal medical attention, all that was missing was a minibar. Patched through to operation HQ at NYPD where a very excited inspector wanted to hear all about it. First of all, however, I had a question for him.

"What day is it?"

"Thursday."

"And when's Marshall's pretrial hearing?"

"Tomorrow morning." He coughed. "If we can find him."

"You mean he's run?"

"We're monitoring all the airports."

"Great." *That's really going to work, isn't it?* "Where's the money?"

"He's shifted a large amount of Marshall Land's capital to an account in Liberia."

"So what's the plan?"

"Well, Major Stagg... We're kind of relying on you."

I returned to Manhattan with more style than I'd left it. Jack Rendell of Parker-Rendell put his vast office at my disposal, and it was here that I received senior officers from New York's finest. I was assigned to the operation as a civilian expert—but nobody objected when I said I wanted to be on the front line. New clothes were waiting for me, chosen and bought by Martin Kingston. I guess it was a guilt-offering; his daughter Linda, a thirtysomething mother of two who lived on Long Island, had never been in the slightest danger, and if he'd bothered to call her before rushing out of the apartment I might have been spared a beating and a armful of whatever shit they shot me up with.

The two immediate objectives were simple: first, secure and detain Julian Marshall, and second, provide sufficient evidence at the pretrial hearing on Friday morning. Simple, but not easy. Marshall had disappeared, the hearing was less than twelve hours away, and the key witness, Jody Miller, alias Brian Cooper, alias Stirling McMahon/McMasters (the list went on) was on a life-support machine in an intensive care unit in Trenton, New Jersey. Of course I could tell the judge what Jody had told me—but that wasn't going to stand up in court. There was the small matter of abduction and torture to discuss—enough, perhaps, to put Enrico Ferrari behind bars for a couple of years. But Marshall had been careful. Nothing connected him to Ferrari; there was no one by that name on the Marshall Land payroll. I had never seen them together. Ferrari never told me who he was working for. Damn it, nobody could even connect him with Trey Peters. Without Jody, and without Marshall, the party was off.

Ferrari was in police custody, but I'd done rather too good a job of smashing his face in to make him much use as a witness just yet. By the time the doctors let him talk to anyone, Marshall would be sitting on a pile of gold somewhere in the tropics. I'm sure the Liberian boys would do very well by him.

New York City is a big place with an awful lot of airports within striking distance. The last confirmed sighting of Julian Marshall was Martin's interview with him the previous Tuesday—the day I'd been hit by a car on the sidewalk, the day of the bogus kidnapping of Martin's daughter and the all-too-real kidnapping of yours truly. Financial records showed that he'd been busy in that time, but it was impossible to say where he was. Marshall Land had gone into lockdown; the staff couldn't even get to their desks on Wednesday morning, and the boss wasn't answering any of his usual phones. His addresses in Manhattan and Connecticut were unoccupied.

A needle in a haystack, then—and short of closing down the entire city we were never going to find him.

So what do you do when the combined forces of law and order can't lay their hands on Public Enemy

Number One? I've had a little experience of this myself, between my service record and some of the hopeless manhunts I've been involved in over the last few years. When you've searched every place you can think of, when your quarry still evades you, you set a trap.

There are three things you need for a trap. Intelligence, to locate your prey and understand its habits. Mechanism, the spring that catches the mouse, the concealed pit that catches the bear, the phalanx of heavily-armed cops that suddenly surrounds the absconding criminal. And last but not least, you need bait.

At the moment we had none of those things, and our only possible informant was lying on an operating table while surgeons attempted to salvage his once-perfect, Italian, movie-star profile. But we had the whole night ahead of us, and the considerable resources of Parker-Rendell at our disposal, and if between us we couldn't produce Julian Marshall in court to face at least some kind of indictment the following morning—well, there's always welfare.

"What does Marshall want more than anything?"

I sat at the head of the long, polished oak table, my back to the vastness of nighttime Manhattan on the other side of the glass wall.

"Money," said Jack Rendell. The cops nodded.

I waggled my hand. "And what does he love almost as much as money?"

There was a certain amount of coughing from around the table. Martin Kingston seemed suddenly interested in his coffee cup, and Jack Rendell scanned the ceiling.

The cops looked baffled.

"Ass," I said. "Young American ass, to be precise.

Preferably blond." Jody had bleached his hair, hadn't he? "And if we assume that he's still somewhere in New York, then I'd guess he's not going anywhere until he's had one last piece."

"What are you suggesting?"

"Where do guys like Julian Marshall go to find company these days?"

"Nightclubs?" said one of the cops. "Bath houses?"

"No way. He's too old for clubs and too recognizable for the baths. Anyway," I said, remembering what Jody had told me, "it's all online now. Right?"

Jack nodded. "So what are we going to do?"

"We're going fishing," I said. "I need an Internet connection and someone who knows how to use the damn thing. And I need you to find me a blond."

"Oh, sure," said Jack, putting his hands behind his head. "It's that easy. We just go out into the street and pick one up."

"Actually," I said, "I was wondering if the NYPD might help us out. Guys?"

It looked to all intents and purposes like a standard lineup, until you saw their faces. Then it looked more like a casting call for an Abercrombie & Fitch campaign. There were six of them standing at ease, all of them in their twenties, all of them in fine physical shape, all of them blond. Some—those who were lucky enough to be on duty when the call came—were in uniform. Three were in civilian clothes, and one of them looked as if he was still in his pajamas, with trainers and a fleece hoodie thrown on.

We were at the 5th Precinct, Martin Kingston, Jack

Rendell, a station sergeant and me, sitting behind a one-way mirror.

"I'll take 'em all," murmured Martin, and I could tell from Jack's frequent clearing of his throat that he was thinking the same. The sergeant didn't turn a hair. Fat and in his fifties, with a wedding band and a seen-it-all-before expression—setting up a cute blond sergeant for a sting was all in a night's work.

All six were handsome as hell. I wondered who exactly was in charge of recruitment these days and wanted to shake that person's hand.

"I'll have to ask them to take their shirts off."

Jack put his hands over his face.

"Why?" asked the sergeant.

"Because Marshall has a type."

The cop shrugged and switched on the intercom. "Okay, guys. Shirts off."

There was a certain amount of laughter and horse-play, but within sixty seconds I had six topless blond cops in front of me. I've had tougher assignments.

"Okay. One, three and four, you can go."

"Are you crazy?" whispered Martin. "I mean…well, number three in particular…"

"I'm sure you can get their names and numbers from the front desk," I said. "The point is, they're hairy."

"Yeah, exactly."

"And Marshall likes 'em smooth. Jody shaved and plucked and god knows what else."

And then there were three.

I pressed the button on the intercom. "Hey, number five."

"Sir?"

"How tall are you?"

"Five eight, sir."

"You can go." He actually looked crestfallen; I had to wonder what exactly their superiors had told them about the job they were "volunteering" for. Jack Rendell made a little groaning noise; I think I'd just eliminated his favorite.

"I'm going in to talk to them."

"Should I come too?" asked Martin, sounding hopeful. I thought on the whole I'd be better on my own. If either of the boys got a look at the front of his pants, they might lose their nerve.

The room was brightly lit with overhead fluorescents and smelled pleasantly of warm young men.

"We don't have very much time," I said in the tone that I'd used in a thousand military briefings, "so I'm going to speak directly. Is either one of you gay?"

"No, sir," said number six.

"And you, sergeant?"

"Will this go on my records, sir?"

"If it does," I said, "I personally undertake to kick the living shit out of the officer who puts it there. So?"

"I've fooled around."

"Much?"

"Quite a bit." He was five eleven, maybe six feet tall, his hair neatly cut and side parted, his skin smooth and pale over a swimmer's body. Smooth, but for a dark treasure trail. Nice pink tits that made me think of clothespins.

"Turn around."

He did as he was told. The kind of ass you could rest a cup of coffee on.

"Go and shave. Be ready in five minutes, understand?"

"Sir."

"Do you need me?" Number six—the one in the PJs—was scratching his head, the muscles in his arm and chest making a nice show under the bright lights.

I could think of a dozen uses for him, but not right now. "You can go home to bed."

I'd like to think the look on his face was disappointment rather than relief.

"What's your name?"

"Eric Johanssen. Officer Eric Johanssen."

"Hmm. Let me think about that."

We were back at Parker-Rendell in a hospitality room that was used by visitors or night-owl executives. It was decked out with a bed, a wardrobe, a chest of drawers and the kind of bland tasteful decor you find in midprice hotels and porn sites. There was a neutral print on the wall, and even a vase with a bunch of sticks in it. I'll never understand that one.

The tech boys had been in as instructed. There was a laptop on the bed and a webcam positioned on the nightstand. Three chairs had been arranged in a semicircle well out of the shot.

"Eric. Hmm. Ricky? No, not preppy enough. Where'd you go to college, Eric?"

"Ithaca."

"No, that won't do. Sounds Greek. Hey, Jack!" Rendell was hovering nervously around the chairs. "Got any ideas for a good high-class hustler name?"

"Channing."

"Perfect. Any particular reason?"

"Oh," he said "I think I just...saw it on a...you know. Website."

Eric—or Channing, as we must now call him—was freshly showered and shaved and wearing a new white terrycloth robe; Parker-Rendell treats its guests well. All he had underneath were box-fresh white Calvin Klein underpants and a pair of white tube socks. Martin had been in charge of the wardrobe for this little production number. Thank god for 24-hour stores.

"Now, you're going to be just fine," said the fat, married sergeant. "I mean we'll be right outside if you need us, okay? Just...outside."

The door closed, leaving one young blond cop facing three older men.

"Make yourself comfortable, then."

Channing jumped up on the bed and tested the bounce. His robe fell open.

"Okay. I'm ready."

"Just remember," said Jack Rendell, "you're on your own. Don't look at us. Forget we're here."

"That's fine."

"Let's get this show on the road, then," I said. "Martin—you sure about these websites?"

"They're the classy ones. High subscription rates, lots of traffic, high-end clientele." Now that the senior cops had left us, he was a lot more relaxed. "If Marshall goes anywhere, he'll go to one of them."

We were set up on three different websites: Manhattan Massage Therapy, Fit for Life Personal Training Exchange, Ivy League Recruitment.

"Okay, go ahead and log on. Remember your username: Channing."

"Sure. Channing." He settled the laptop on his thighs and tapped the keyboard. We watched on a monitor as he flipped between tabs. "Okay. I'm in."

"Get the camera on. Remember, no sound."

"Give me a moment." The cursor flashed around the screen, clicking on boxes, and a picture appeared in the bottom right-hand corner of the screen. Channing adjusted the camera until he was satisfied with the framing. He lay back and ran a hand over his stomach. "Okay. Showtime."

A volley of pings from the speakers. Channing was popular. Channing was new. Channing was lying back in an open robe with a handsome bulge in his briefs. The greater New York area was sitting up and taking notice—even in the small hours.

"Hey, guys," typed Channing. "Just got back from the gym."

Ping! Ping! Ping!

Like I said, all this online stuff is unfamiliar territory to me. Channing, however, seemed right at home. I guess he'd done it before. Martin and Jack exchanged approving glances.

We watched the conversation on the monitor, and watched Channing on the bed.

- Hey channing looking good dude
- Yo chan sup horny here
- Me 2 man anyone need a massage

More and more windows popped up, the dialogue

flowing as fast as credits at the end of a movie. None of it made any sense to me. And then:

- Good evening, Channing. I wonder if you're available at the moment?

"That last one," I said. "Say hi to him." It was properly spelled and punctuated, and I didn't quite see Marshall using words like "dude" and "sup."

The username? "SilverMan." "That means he's the right age," whispered Martin, pointing to his hair.

- Hi SilverMan. Sure, I'm free. What you up to?
- Just relaxing in my hotel room.
- Nice. Late night? J
- No—early morning, in fact. Flight to catch.

"That's him. It's got to be him."

"It could be anyone," said Jack. "You can't just assume..."

"Got any better ideas?" I realized that I was snarling, but I was desperate for this to work. "Channing, ask him for a photo."

"No!" Jack almost jumped out of his seat; Channing, thank god, kept his cool and didn't even look at us, just lay there on the bed rubbing his tight, smooth abdomen. "You'll scare him off. Guys like him never show their photos. It's a one-way deal."

"Okay. Just chat to him."

- Going somewhere nice?
- Just a business trip. Long haul. Could do with a massage

to set me up before I go.
- Sure—travel or accom?

I looked to Martin for translation.

"He's trying to find out if SilverMan will come here, or wants him to go there."

"Jesus," I said, "he can't come here!"

"Don't worry. Our boy knows what he's doing."

Channing rearranged himself on the bed, allowing his robe to fall open a little more.

- Would you mind coming here?
- No problem. You in Manhattan?
- Yes.
- Cool.

"Why doesn't he ask him for the address?"

"All in good time. You can't rush him. SilverMan has to trust him first."

"And how's he going to get him to do that?"

"Watch and learn, Dan. Watch and learn." Martin nodded toward the bed, where Channing was fiddling with the waistband of his briefs.

- You seem to be in very good shape, Channing.
- I do my best.
- What would you be wearing when you do the massage?
- Usually just my shorts.

He pulled the elastic down a little.

- I see.

If ever letters on a screen communicated disappointment, they did.

- But I can work naked if you prefer J
- That would be very nice.
- Yeah for me too. Prefer being naked.
- Oh, really?
- J

Channing removed his arms from the sleeves of his robe,
exposing his torso. I don't know about "SilverMan," but
the three guys in the room with Channing were getting
very hard. If this little sting didn't work, maybe we'd
just lock the door and take turns fucking Channing in
the mouth and ass.

- Very nice.
- Thanks.
- What kind of massage do you specialize in?

Specialize, indeed. If I had Channing on the end of a
webcam I'd have other things on my mind than massage
techniques, but I guess guys like Marshall—sorry,
SilverMan—need to keep up the pretense.

- Swedish, reiki, shiatsu, tantric
- Ah, tantric?
- You like?
- Yes very much.

I thought "shiatsu" was a fancy breed of dog, and as
for tantric... I looked over at Jack, who made a jerk-off

gesture with his hand. Ah, that. Not what I call it, but I get the picture.

- Great. Want me to come over?
- Just one thing—would you mind turning over for me?
- No problem. Want to see what yr getting?
- Yes please.

"Got you."

Channing was a natural performer. He got up on his knees—there was a definite bulge in his shorts now, and he made sure the camera got a good look—then turned around, looking over his shoulder to check that he was properly framed. It was as tight and round as any of us could desire. In this position, obviously, he couldn't type. SilverMan could, however.

- Very nice. You obviously take good care of yourself. So many young men of your age let themselves go. It's important to keep healthy and fit. Not just in the body but in the mind as well. I'm a great believer in a healthy mind in a healthy body. Oh, my god.

In between each of these statements Channing gave encouragement by rubbing his asscheeks, pulling the sides of his briefs up to expose his buttocks, and rolling the waistband down. The final *Oh, my god* came when he pulled them down altogether. I've seen some fine asses lately, but Channing—Officer Eric Johannsen, NYPD—takes the gold medal. He smacked himself smartly on the right buttock; the flesh quivered, and a pink handprint quickly developed on the pale skin.

As a final gesture, he pulled the cheeks apart and gave SilverMan (and the three of us) a quick flash of his rosebud hole. We all sighed.

Channing flipped over and sat down with a bounce.

- You like?
- Very much. So how much for a massage please?
- $350. That okay? As long as you're below 72nd otherwise cab fare on top J
- That's fine, I'm in Midtown.
- Great. Can be with you in 20 mins. Address?

There followed a long pause. Had Channing overplayed his hand? Had SilverMan suddenly got cold feet? We waited. Channing carried on stroking his abs. Nothing. Shit! We'd lost him.

And then Channing pulled his underpants right down and gave us all a view of his dick.

- The Time. 49th near Broadway. Meet in lobby in 20mins okay?
- On my way.

He gave the camera one final heartbreaking smile and closed the lid of the laptop. "Channing" was no more. We had one naked blond police officer in his early twenties, stark naked with a hard-on, blushing and grinning at three very horny middle-aged men who were finding it difficult to keep their minds on the job.

"How was I, guys?"

There was no time for compliments. "You did well. Get dressed. The car's waiting."

The Time hotel has the kind of security that you don't notice until you try to get into the elevator without being announced. There's a beautiful young woman on the reception desk and a couple of bellhops hovering near the concierge desk in the shadows—and there are surveillance cameras covering every inch of the lobby. In order to access any of the guests, you have to be scrutinized by a video security phone. Every room has a full closed-circuit-TV view of the lobby. It could have been designed with absconding criminals in mind.

In the good old days we'd have busted into the lobby, flashed our badges and swarmed up the stairs to the relevant floor, maybe posting a couple of men on the fire escape in case our quarry tried anything daring. Marshall was too smart for that kind of approach. He'd chosen a final refuge that was hermetically sealed against intruders.

We parked a block back from the entrance. Marshall might be watching the street; he might even have guards posted around the hotel area. Sounds overcautious, perhaps, but there was no point in risking a gunfight if we could avoid it.

A single plainclothes officer went in to talk to the receptionist; if we made a commotion, our bird would fly. Once he'd explained, quietly and calmly, that the Time was now the site of a police operation and that her help would be "appreciated," we released "Channing" onto the street. I watched his ass in grey stretch jersey bouncing toward the posh entrance of the hotel.

"Okay, he's in."

And now we waited. In ten minutes—by which time we expected Marshall's attention might have wandered from the security monitors to the more pleasant view of Channing's white ass and rose pink hole—we would follow him upstairs in the elevator and make our arrest.

All quiet on 49th Street. Nobody running, no cars screeching to a halt in front of the Time, no shouting or gunfire. Ten minutes passed. The five of us moved noiselessly across the lobby.

"Room 405."

"What's the name?"

"Joseph Thorne."

Shit—not SilverMan, and not, obviously, Marshall. We still had no sure way of knowing that we had the right man. Could just be some unfortunate random rich guy with an early morning flight and a taste for bubble-butted blond trade. City must be full of 'em.

The night manager let us into the elevator and reluctantly handed over a keycard. He looked furious, and on the verge of tears.

If Marshall had booked into a cheaper hotel—somewhere like the place my trick from the Downtown Diner took me, for instance—the plan would have worked like a charm. The NYPD is good at breaking down doors. But the Time was just a little too well designed for that.

We flanked the door, two on each side. Solid dark brown wood—teak or mahogany or something like that, but it might as well have been veneered steel. No amount of kicking was going to bring that sucker down. Even shooting the lock was out of the question. Our only option was to use the keycard, and hope that Marshall— if it was Marshall—was so engrossed in Channing's ass that he wouldn't hear us until it was too late. According to Jody he was interested in spanking. That should provide some distraction—but would it be enough?

We held our breath and listened. Nothing penetrated that door. Channing could be screaming bloody murder and we'd be none the wiser.

Softly, so softly, the cop slid the card into the look. The light flashed up red, and then green. A soft click, a gentle push and the door was open.

The room was empty. Nobody on the bed, nobody in the armchair, over the table, swinging from the light fittings. No sign of occupation at all.

Wait. A flash of white. Channing's box-fresh briefs scrunched up and thrown under the dressing table.

The bathroom. It was the only possibility.

The door was closed. I tried the handle. Locked. No pass key. The time for surprise had passed. Now came the negotiation, and with it a significantly decreased chance of success. Channing was in jeopardy.

"Julian Marshall." The cop's voice sounded loud in the well-upholstered room. "Open the door. This is the police."

Nothing. No sounds of a scuffle, no voices.

Had Marshall been warned, and fled? And where was Channing?

"Marshall!" He knocked on the door, four loud bangs.

Nothing.

"Okay, stand back. I'm going to shoot the lock."

He cocked his pistol and aimed at the lock.

The burnished steel door handle moved slowly, smoothly down. The cop put up his weapon.

The first thing we saw through the gap was Channing's pale naked leg, then his hip, his waist, and as the door opened further, the glint of metal as Marshall pressed the barrel of a gun against the boy's temple. One fat finger was curled around the trigger.

"One move and I shoot the little bastard." His voice was low and calm.

"Put the gun down, Mr. Marshall," said the cop.

He didn't deny the identification. "Stand aside and let me pass."

"I can't do that, sir."

"You surely don't think I'm joking, do you?"

The cops looked at each other, and stepped back. Pushing the scared, naked boy in front of him, Marshall—fat, fully dressed, sports jacket and tie— walked out of the bathroom.

"Here's the deal, gentlemen. You will leave the way you came in. In precisely two minutes, I will walk through that door and I will leave the hotel. If I even suspect that any of you is still on the premises, I will kill him. Do you understand me?"

"Sir, please listen to me..."

"Don't try the bargaining bullshit. I read the psychology books, too. Now just get the fuck out of my room before I put a bullet through this little whore's brain."

"If you put the gun down..."

"Ten," said Marshall. "Nine. Eight..."

The gun pushed the skin up on Channing's temple. His face was white, his lips blue, his cock shrunk to a tiny wrinkle of flesh.

The NYPD probably likes to play things by the

book these days. Certainly, the odds were against us; Marshall looked like he meant business, and there was no way they would consider sacrificing one of their own in order to secure the objective.

However, they had made the operational misjudgment of allowing a civilian to accompany them—a civilian with military experience.

I positioned myself at the back of the line that was filing politely out of Marshall's room.

"Keep walking, guys." A mocking, sarcastic note in his voice—good, he thinks he's beaten us. Let him think he's won.

One cop out, two cops out, three, four.

I turned in the doorway and took my cap off.

"I don't think we've been properly introduced, Mr. Marshall. My name's Stagg. Dan Stagg."

It took him a second to remember the name, and then his lips opened to say something—a bubble of spit formed at the side of his mouth—but I guess I'd run out of patience. I knew one key fact about Julian Marshall—he gets other people to do his dirty work for him, cold-hearted thugs like Ferrari. He doesn't get his hands dirty; he's not used to pulling the trigger and seeing the consequences. He's playing a good hand—he knows how to get his own way—but he might hesitate before carrying out his threat. And that gave me time. Not much time, admittedly, but how long does it take?

Marshall was twice as wide as the naked cop he was holding in front of him, but even so I couldn't get a clean line on him. But people make a common mistake when they use a human shield. They forget that a really experienced opponent will think in terms of acceptable levels of injury. Channing was going to get hurt—but he was not going to get killed. And he presented one hell of a target—a long, lean, smooth torso of ivory flesh.

A simple but direct side kick to Channing's solar plexus, the impact coming from the outer edge of the foot, and he doubled over, cannoning backward with his ass. Marshall didn't let go—he still had an arm locked around Channing's neck—but Marshall was temporarily off balance and, crucially, the gun was away from Channing's head, waving in the air as Marshall sought his footing. That was all it took. I grabbed his wrist and pushed it backward, pressing my thumb as hard as possible between the tendons at the base of his hand. He screamed and fell to the floor. I wedged my knee under the elbow of his gun arm and smashed down hard with my elbow, shattering the joint.

Channing fell behind me, fighting for breath.

The gun was clear. I kicked it out of reach, just to be on the safe side.

The police swarmed back into the room—four burly officers to overpower one flabby old man. I rolled Channing on to his side, pulled the cover off the bed and waited for the medics to arrive.

"You okay?"

The color was returning to his face.

"Sh...sure..."

"We got him."

"G...g..."

He vomited on to the carpet.

Enrico Ferrari was no longer the movie star who walked into my room on 109th Street a week and a half ago. His face was a mass of scars and bruises, one eye closed to a purple slit, his left cheek swelled out like a baseball and his lovely dark floppy hair shaved up the side of his head to make way for an unattractive rail-road of stitches.

The doctors were reluctant to let us in to interview him until the scale of Ferrari's offences was pointed out as well as the urgency of putting together enough evidence to satisfy the pretrial hearing. "All yours, gentlemen," said the nurse, holding the door open.

There were three of us: me, a sergeant, and an inspector from the Organized Crime Control Bureau. Unfortunately we weren't there for a hospital-bed orgy. Yes, they were both hot: Sergeant Lynskey was short, bald and blue eyed, Inspector Rotherstein was a little older than me, grey haired and athletic. They knew enough about my involvement in the case to realize that, given opportunity and a door with a lock, I'll fuck anything in pants—but I guess they had other things on their mind. And for once, so did I.

Ferrari grimaced when he saw me. "What's he doing here?"

"Major Stagg," said Inspector Rotherstein, "is assigned to this investigation."

"You can't do that."

"Watch me," said Rotherstein.

"I want a lawyer."

"And you have every right to one. But before we get all official on you, we just wanted to have a friendly chat. Off the record, so to speak."

"I've got nothing to say."

"Let me appeal to your better nature, Mr. Ferrari. You see, we want the best possible chance of getting a conviction against Julian Marshall."

"Who?"

Rotherstein smiled. "Your evidence would be so valuable to us."

Ferrari looked away.

"Wouldn't you like to bring a major criminal to justice, Mr. Ferrari?"

"I told you, I want legal representation."

"I'd have thought Mr. Marshall would be providing that for you. His trusted lieutenant."

"Don't know what you're talking about."

"Really? Julian Marshall, of Marshall Land? Doesn't that name ring a bell?"

Ferrari shrugged.

"His number is on your phone. Why don't you call him and ask him to remind you who he is?"

Ferrari started to speak, but thought better of it.

"That's right—of course! You mislaid your phone, right? I expect you've been worrying about it. It's a nice phone. But it's okay, Mr. Ferrari. We found it."

"Huh."

"I thought you'd be pleased." Rotherstein produced the phone from his pocket—a sleek, black oblong with a large screen. "Phones these days! They do everything, don't they? Make calls, send texts, tell the time, do your shopping for you. Take pictures."

A pause. Ferrari stared at his water carafe.

"Even moving pictures."

Silence.

"Amazing, isn't it?"

Ferrari shifted in his bed and winced in pain. He looked like a kid who's been caught with his hand in the cookie jar.

"Now, Mr. Ferrari, you see why I wanted to keep this all friendly and informal. There's enough on this camera to put you away for—oh, let me see—ten, fifteen years? And that's without anything that might come up in the Marshall trial. Because he will come to trial, with or without your cooperation. Thing is, if you wanted to help us, you'd be helping yourself. We might just accidentally wipe some of the home movies on your clever little cell phone. Major Stagg here might develop a touch of amnesia about what you did to him in that warehouse. I mean, he was unconscious for most of the time, wasn't he? Can't be expected to remember everything. A good defense attorney would say he'd dreamed the whole thing. As for Mr. Cooper..."

"Who?"

"Oh, I'm sorry. You probably know him as Stirling

McMahon." Rotherstein made great show of referring to his notes. "You know. The one you abducted and raped?"

"Huh."

"And filmed."

Ferrari crossed his arms over his chest. The hospital pajamas really weren't doing him any favors.

"What was the big idea, Ferrari? Something to jerk off to in your old age? A new career in Internet porn? Come on. What kind of asshole leaves evidence like this lying around? Someone who wants to get caught, I'd say. Wouldn't you, Major Stagg?"

"Someone with a dirty little secret," I said.

"So what's the story?" Rotherstein perched on the edge of the bed. "You were Marshall's delivery boy, weren't you? Surely there was plenty to go around. Or didn't the boss like you sampling the goods?"

"Fuck you."

"You can play the macho gangster all you like, Ferrari, but this says different." Rotherstein gently slapped the cell phone against the palm of his hand. "What's your defense going to be? Plenty to choose from, and I've heard 'em all. How about good old homosexual panic? When confronted with a gay man you totally lost your mind and started raping and kidnapping. Hmm, but that doesn't account for some of the stuff we saw. Okay, let's try undue influence. 'Julian Marshall brainwashed me with his perverted habits and I couldn't control myself.' So in a fit of temporary insanity you forced a semiconscious man to fuck Stirling McMahon for the cameras before you proceeded to beat the shit out of both of them in—what? An attack of guilt?"

"Listen…"

Rotherstein held up his hand. "Or try this for size. You were abused as a kid by—hey, is Ferrari an Italian name? You were abused by priests, then. You struggled for years against it but then it all came flooding back and you had to reenact it as a form of therapy. That could get you off, with the right judge. You might even sue the Roman Catholic church for damages. What do you say?"

"Listen, man…"

"I'm all ears."

Ferrari made a few false starts. "I don't know."

"How about I ask you some questions, and you give me some answers? Crazy idea. But let's just try it."

Sergeant Lynskey and I sat down to watch the show.

"Now, Mr. Ferrari." Rotherstein looked out of the window as if intrigued by the dismal view. "Let's go back to the events of last Friday, shall we? Not too far back. Can you remember where you were, and what you were doing?"

"Of course I can't."

"No, you're a busy man. Why should you remember every little detail? So let me help you. Major Stagg here called you just after midday. You didn't answer your phone."

"For fuck's sake."

"You spoke later in the day, around about five. Yes? You told Major Stagg you'd been on the subway."

"That's right."

"Take the subway often, Mr. Ferrari?"

"No."

"Good." Rotherstein turned toward the bed with an affable smile. "So you'll doubtless remember the occasion. Like, where you were going, what you were doing."

"I don't know."

"Could it be, in fact, that you made a mistake? You hadn't been in the subway at all. That was just the first thing you could think up to explain why you didn't answer Major Stagg's call."

"What the fuck is this all about? You said you were going to ask me questions."

"I'm sorry. I get sidetracked by the details. That's the trouble in my job. The details." He stared down at Ferrari, who seemed to shrink. "Go on."

"What?"

"Friday. Subway, missed phone call, blah, blah, blah. Anything to add?"

"I told you, I want my lawyer."

"Okay. Have it your way. Ten to fifteen for abduction and aggravated sexual assault. I think I've got enough to get a couple of conspiracy charges to stick. You'll be popular in jail, Ferrari." Rotherstein slapped his forehead, as if something obvious had just occurred to him. "Of course! That's what you want, isn't it? I guess you'd like nothing more than to be locked up with half a dozen giant psychopaths who haven't seen a pussy for years."

That took the wind out of Ferrari's sails. "I was with Marshall, okay? Friday. We had a...meeting."

"Ah." Rotherstein sat on the bed, the concerned father once more. "Now we're getting somewhere. Why don't you tell us what that meeting was about?"

"I can't remember."

"Don't waste my time, Ferrari. You play ball, we'll see what we can do. But I'm losing my patience. Do you understand me?"

Ferrari understood. "Marshall was planning to leave the country."

"Lynskey, take notes."

"That was never in the plan. I was supposed to get Stirling out of town while the cops were trying to talk to him, that's all."

"And what then? He was going to have a little accident on the road?"

"No!" shouted Ferrari, then clutched his jaw in pain. "No. He was going to be paid off, sent away. I swear to god."

Rotherstein caught my eye; he knew all about our late-night visitor in the Starlight Motel. "So what happened? Why did the plans change?"

"Marshall panicked. He knew that the investigation was closing in on him. Even without Stirling's evidence, he was fucked."

"So he decided to run."

"Yeah. Suddenly he had this meeting that was going to take him out of town for a couple of days. I didn't trust him. That's why I didn't pick up the phone. I was in his office. I told him that I was nervous about him leaving town because if he wasn't around, I was going to face the music for...you know."

"Trey Peters?"

"I didn't kill him."

"No one's suggesting you did. Go on."

"I told Marshall he had better make sure I didn't start talking to the cops, know what I mean?"

"You blackmailed him."

"Severance pay, that's what it was. He owed me. I'd done stuff for him that... Well, extra stuff."

"But he didn't pay up?"

"He told me I'd have it by three o'clock."

"Let me guess..."

"I don't like to be kept waiting."

"Tough guy."

"So if Marshall was going to screw me, I was going to screw him. That's when I decided to bring Stirling back to New York City."

"You... What?" Even Rotherstein didn't see that one coming.

"I made a few calls. Found a guy I could trust up in New Hampshire. And when Stagg phoned in with the details of where they were staying, I sent him in to collect the goods."

"Bullshit, Ferrari," I said. "He had a gun pointed at my head."

"I warned him that you might be trouble. He wasn't taking any chances."

"So what was the plan?" continued Rotherstein. "You were going to ask Mr. Cooper...sorry, Stirling to accompany this friend of yours back to New York City so that he could apply pressure to Julian Marshall?"

"I was going to deliver him to you guys if Marshall didn't pay up."

"That's crap," I said. "It was a hit."

Rotherstein silenced me with a look. "You took control of the mission at this point, Mr. Ferrari?"

"Yeah."

"And what happened?"

"You know what happened. Stagg nearly killed my guy."

"Indeed."

"And we lost them somewhere in the mountains."

"You expect us to believe that you managed to track Major Stagg to Buffalo?"

Ferrari laughed. "Hey—that was the easy part. You were careless, Stagg."

I went over the journey in my mind—Kenny and Pete the Cop in the woods, Bill and Hank in the gas station bathroom, our final stop in Buffalo. Who had betrayed us?

"You picked Stirling up in Buffalo and took him directly to the warehouse in Trenton, New Jersey?"

"Marshall had disappeared. Nobody knew where he was. I had to keep Stirling safe."

"I wouldn't say he was safe with you, Mr. Ferrari. Not judging by the condition in which Major Stagg found him."

"We were going to hide up there until we knew where Marshall was. The warehouse..."

"Belongs to your cousin. We know."

"No one at Marshall Land knew where he was. The offices were closed. Time was running out."

"So why didn't you put the whole matter into the hands of the police?"

"Don't be stupid, man."

Rotherstein raised his eyebrows by an eighth of an inch. He obviously didn't like being called stupid. "Surely you realized by that time that Marshall was out of your reach? If you were intending to blackmail... sorry, to persuade him to pay you the money he owed, you'd missed your chance. Stirling McMahon's evidence was of no further use to you. In fact, far from being useful, he was a danger. He could put you behind bars as well as Marshall."

"That's crap."

"How else can I explain what happened to him in that warehouse, Ferrari? You tortured him and left him for dead. If that wasn't a way of silencing him, what was it?"

No comment from Mr. Ferrari.

"You see, time and time again we come up against this mystery. Why would a tough guy like Enrico Ferrari suddenly start fooling around with Stirling McMahon? Why would he want to film him getting fucked up the ass by Major Stagg here? And why did he then attempt to... What was it, Major Stagg? What did he try to do to you?"

I caught Ferrari's eye and smiled.

Enrico Ferrari testified in the pretrial hearing against Julian Marshall. The judge was satisfied that there was enough evidence to charge Marshall in the death of Trey Peters, and a full-scale police inquiry into the business methods of Marshall Land began. Immediately after the hearing, Ferrari was charged with abduction and assault. He complained to anyone who would listen that he'd been set up by the cops. He was ignored.

It seemed like a pretty good result. Then I learned that Jody had suffered a brain hemorrhage.

The message went from the hospital to the NYPD to Jack Rendell to Martin Kingston. It was Martin who told me.

I sat in his apartment in Morningside Heights crying like a baby.

"This changes everything," said Martin, trying to comfort me. "They'll throw the book at Ferrari. They'll charge him with attempted murder, or..."

"I don't care about Ferrari!" God, I hate the sound of my voice when I'm crying. I don't hear it that often. Twice, three times in my adult life. When Will died. When I broke down in the disciplinary hearing. Now. "If he dies..."

I couldn't go on; something big was trying to burst out of my chest. My heart, I guess.

Martin went to the kitchen and fixed a sandwich. He understood the value of food at times like this. We ate in silence.

"I don't know what to do," I said when I'd finished.

"You're going to go to him."

"What's the point?"

Martin said nothing, just looked at me. I wanted to run.

"Look," he said, "I'd like nothing better than to keep you for myself. I could lock you up in the apartment, let you out once in a while to go to the gym, and spend the rest of the time fucking that sweet marine ass of yours."

At least that made me smile.

"But that wouldn't be right for you, would it?"

"Martin..."

"You know what's right for you."

"How can I just turn up in the hospital... I'm nothing to him. What can I do? I mean...he's..."

"Dying? Maybe. And if you don't go, you'll never

know what might have happened."

"I can't help."

"Yes, you can." I blew my nose and waited for him to explain. "There's a chance that all that stuff you said to each other on the road—all the things you told me about—might actually have been true. You might love him."

"Oh, for god's sake."

"And he might love you. Stranger things have happened."

"Guys like Jody don't love guys like me."

"They trained you well in the marines, didn't they, Dan? Made you believe all the bullshit."

"I can't do it, Martin. I can't just..."

"Pack a bag. Be ready in ten minutes. I'll drive."

Another car, another highway, another mission with little chance of success. Destination? Trenton, New Jersey, of course.

Jody was recovering from emergency brain surgery in the intensive care ward. "You can't go up now unless you're family," said the receptionist.

"I'm not family."

"Then come back at five."

It was two o'clock in the afternoon. Three hours in which to decide that this was a waste of time, to run away, to blot it all out with drink or sex and return to New York City to wait for the next disappointment.

They trained you well, didn't they? Made you believe all the bullshit.

Martin was right, damn him. I believed that guys like me go through life without attachments, making tactical decisions, watching our backs. I let my guard down once with Will Laurence, and it cost me my career, my status, my self-respect. For what? For the kind of sex I could get any night of the week, as long as I keep myself in shape.

And then what? Forty bucks on the nightstand? Until the day when the wrinkles are deeper and the flesh is saggier and I'm the one who has to pay for it, what then? You can't afford much on a doorman's wages. Rent—just about. Food—if you're careful. Sex? Forget it. Junk food and jerking off, that was the future I was looking at. Not much of a prospect for a man who'd served his country for twelve years.

Come back at five...

Two and three-quarter hours.

And what would I find if I went back at five? Jody/Brian/Stirling, whoever and whatever he was, a cute guy with a great ass and brain damage. What could he offer me? What could I possibly offer him? We'd known each other for a week and a half, we'd fucked in various positions throughout New England, and we'd been caught up in the violent endgame of a massive organized crime operation. Not exactly the basis for enduring love, is it?

They trained you well...

Fuck off, Kingston! Get out of my head! What the fuck was his problem? Pissed off because Jack Rendell got the cute blond cop, not him? Taking it out on me, because he knew I wasn't going to stick around as his bottom boy? Yeah, get back to the steam room, Martin, and wave your wiener at someone else. I've had enough.

Made you believe all the bullshit.

"Fuck!" I was walking down the street outside the hospital, talking to myself. Great. Now I was a loony. Check yourself in, Dan, why don't you? I'm sure they have a psychiatric ward. See if they can give you some happy pills. Take a fucking overdose while you're at it. Do everyone a favor.

They trained you well.

A hundred times I was ready to leave. A hundred times I walked back to the hospital entrance, checking my watch, pacing up and down and wishing for a miracle, a sign.

What would Will want me to do?

Clouds part, Will's face appears in the misty distance, birds sing, flutes and violins...

I waited. No message from Will.

"Will is dead."

Talking to yourself again, Stagg. Do much more of that and they'll put you in a straitjacket.

But yes, Will is dead, and I'm alive, and this whole fucking mess isn't going to alter that fact. He died and I was left to face the world without him. And I made a pretty poor job of it.

I saw an ambulance arrive, a stretcher coming out of the back, a body under a blanket with drips in the arms. Some poor bastard who wasn't going to have the luxury of deciding what to do with the rest of his life. Someone who'd had that choice taken away from him.

Ten to five. Ten minutes early. Shit—live with it.

I walked through reception and straight into the elevator.

"Brian Cooper," I said to the nurse on the ward desk.

She smiled, checked her watch and said, "That's okay. He's in there."

A door with a round window through which I could see the corner of a bed.

I pushed the door open. There was a man sitting beside the bed. He was leaning his elbows on his knees, slumped forward in an attitude of exhaustion. I stepped forward enough to see that he was holding Jody's hand in his.

I turned to go, but he heard me, and looked around. "Hi."

"Sorry to disturb you," I said. "I got the wrong..."

"You here to see him? You a friend?"

"Er...yeah. I guess."

He stood up, and I could see Jody's sleeping face, still badly bruised and cut, but recognizable.

"I'm Steve Cooper," he said, holding his hand out. He was tall, well built, a little older than me I guess. Unshaven. Hadn't slept in a while.

"Dan Stagg." We shook, man to man. Rivals? "I guess you're a...a friend too."

"No," said Steve, with a smile. "I'm his dad."

"His dad?"

"He was asking for you."

We alternated watches around Jody's bed, one off, one on, sometimes meeting for long enough to drink a cup of coffee or eat a doughnut. If there was any news, we passed it on. Usually there was nothing. He was "stable," that's what the doctors said, and neither of us asked more. Would he ever wake up? What would he be if he did? How much damage had been done? We wanted to know, and we didn't want to know, and in that state of ignorance four days went by.

Steve was a quiet kind of guy. Didn't talk much about his son, didn't have a lot of questions about me, who I was, what I meant to Jody, what Jody meant to me. And yes—he called him Jody. "His granddaddy's name was Joseph. We gave him that as a second name. Always called him that as a kid. Joe, Jody. Guess it stuck." So—Brian Joseph Cooper. At last he had a name. Mother's name was Miller, married to Steve Cooper "for a while" before she took off. Of her whereabouts, alive or dead, he said nothing. Those stories of growing up with a druggy mom in Michigan, or her various "boyfriends" who put him to work—truth or lies? Who knew what memories were inside his head as it rested motionless on the pillow? Was there anything left, or was it wiped clean? Was there still such a person as Brian Joseph Cooper, or just a body to be fed and washed?

I kept telling myself that I was wasting my time, that there was no point sitting by his bed day after day, waiting for a miracle. Miracles don't happen to guys like Dan Stagg. Dan Stagg loses everything he cares about. And he doesn't have so much to care about in the first place.

Go do what you're good at, Dan. Killing and losing.

But I kept coming back.

On the evening of the fourth day, Steve and I went to a crummy bar in Trenton and got drunk. We were both staying in cheap hotels, and at that point anything seemed better than listening to the life-support machine, or another evening alone in a rented room. So we drank beers and talked about our lives. I told him my service record. He told me about working in the auto industry. I mentioned that I grew up in Massachusetts; he said that he'd been there on holiday once. We both had sisters who were school teachers. We managed a basic level of sports talk. By the time we got to the third beer, we were running out of subjects. Thank god for alcohol.

"Marine, huh."

Here we go again—another trot around the more obvious theaters of conflict of the last couple of decades. Yes, Afghanistan really was as bad as it sounds. Yes, Saddam was a motherfucker. "Uh-huh."

Steve nodded, drank, wiped his mouth. "Didn't know they took guys like you in the marines."

Shit. Didn't see that one coming. "They didn't."

"So why'd you join?"

"Didn't think about it when I was eighteen."

"But you knew, right?"

"I guess."

"You one of them that goes both ways?"

Where was this leading? Surely not... "No, sir." I shook my head. "Never was much interested in girls."

"Okay." More beer. "Like Jody."

"Yeah. Like Jody."

The TV burbled on in the background. I was grateful for that.

"So why did you... No, it's none of my business."

"Go on."

"Why did you join up? If you couldn't...you know."

"That's a question I've asked a lot in the last few years, Steve."

"Yeah." He signaled the barman for more beers. "Guess we all fuck up." Beer came, we drank. "I been married three times."

"Three? Jesus."

"Yep. Each one was *the* one. Each one fucked me over."

"I'm sorry."

"His mama was the first. Real teen queen, you know? Got pregnant when she was eighteen. She told me it was mine—and I guess it could have been. So I did the decent thing. But I couldn't give her what she wanted. She left us when Jody was four."

"Okay."

"My second wife didn't much take to him. He started running away. Detroit, Chicago with his friends. Didn't come home much anymore. My third wife...she was one of those women who got religion, and she wanted to reform us. Stop me drinking. Stop Jody from being what he was. I got sick of it after a while." He drank, shrugged. "So here I am."

"Yup." We clinked bottlenecks. "Here we are."

"Got my boy back, though."

"Yeah." *What's left of him...*

"You going to stick around, Dan? You know, when he's better."

"I don't know."

"Then why're you here?"

"I guess I feel responsible."

"Responsible." He looked at the TV. "Responsible."

Damn him, damn Martin, damn everyone telling me what to do and making me feel bad. Damn Jody, for that matter. Damn Will. Damn the lot of them.

"If Jody..."

Steve looked up. "What?"

"If he wants me to stay."

"He wants you to stay."

"He actually told you that?"

"About all he did tell me. Before..." He tapped the side of his head. "You know."

"Okay." A future sketched itself out in my mind before I could stop it—Jody and me setting up home together, getting jobs, a couple of dogs, a yard full of goldenrod and joe-pye weed, wood to chop for the winter...

"Okay what?" Steve was staring hard.

"If that's what Jody wants then...I guess I'd better do it."

Steve's cell phone rang. It was the hospital. Everything—the bar, the TV sound, that fleeting vision of the future, the hope that Steve had given me—everything collapsed, condensed into that small jangling box with its flashing screen.

"Steve Cooper... yeah... Uh-huh... When?... Okay. Yes, I understand. Thanks for letting me know."

He stared into space for a while.

I was sure Jody was dead.

"That was the nurse," he said at last.

"Yes."

"Jody just came around."

"What?"

"Only for a short while. But he woke up and he talked. He's...he's not going to die, Dan. He's going to be okay."

And we stood at that bar in each other's arms and cried.

Steve Cooper lived in a small, two-bedroom row house in Ann Arbor, Michigan. "It's a dump," he warned me as we drove up there, Jody wrapped in blankets and sleeping in the backseat. "Needs a lot of fixing up. I never seem to have time." He wasn't kidding. It looked like he moved in and never unpacked, certainly never cleaned. We got Jody upstairs to bed in Steve's room, Steve moved his things into what he called the "guest room," a mountain of cardboard boxes and black plastic sacks under which he said there was a mattress, and I camped downstairs on the sofa. It would have been fine, except there was something living in that sofa that liked to bite.

Steve went out to work every morning at eight, came home twelve to fourteen hours later depending on how much beer he drank; I don't think he felt comfortable being around the house with his son's lover who was so close to his age. He never made me feel unwelcome; he was grateful for the care I gave Jody and acknowledged my attempts at home improvements with a nod and a grunt. I put up shelves, mended leaking faucets, replaced the unsanitary kitchen linoleum, washed and scrubbed and vacuumed until the place was no longer a health hazard. I even cooked—nothing fancy, but at least there was always food in the fridge. I did everything for Jody that the visiting nurses didn't do: I washed and fed him, I gave him clean clothes, and got him to and from the bathroom. One day Jody asked me if he could walk up and down the hallway; I put his arm around my shoulders and helped him every step of the way. The next day he did it again, and the next day a little further. Within two weeks of leaving the hospital, he could climb the stairs unassisted. Within three, we were taking short walks up and down the street.

There was a bench on the corner where we could sit in the sun until he was ready to go back. Sometimes I got him a coffee from the cafe across the road, but I didn't like to take my eyes off him for too long.

We hadn't really talked yet.

"When will they interview me?"

It was the first time he'd referred to the investigation of Marshall Land and the charges against Enrico

Ferrari. The police were holding off until Jody was well enough to travel to New York.

"Don't worry about that."

"I'm not worried." He took a deep breath. "I want to do it."

"Okay."

"I'm frightened though."

"You've got nothing to worry about."

"Not that." He waved his hand dismissively. "I'm worried about you."

"Me?"

"When you find out the truth."

A bus rumbled past, a few cars.

"You don't know much about me, Dan."

"I know enough."

"I lied."

"Jody, it's…"

"No." He put his hand on mine. It was thin and pale like the rest of him. He was no longer the pneumatic little gym bunny who first bounced up to me sucking on a straw in Penn Station. His cheeks were hollow, his ass was flat, his hair limp and badly in need of cutting. "Don't stop me. I lied about who I am and what happened to me. I made up stuff to make myself sound more interesting."

"Like going to prison at the age of 14?"

"Yeah. That kind of thing."

"Believe me, Jody, I'd prefer it if you weren't a jail-bird."

"Stuff about my parents. I mean, they got divorced, but I never lost touch with my dad. And stuff about Julian Marshall."

"You weren't an escort?"

"Oh, that was all true. Not the stuff about trying to be an actor; the only acting I've ever done was in fourth grade, and I was hopeless. I wasn't much good as a hustler either. But I got lucky with Marshall." He laughed, and clutched his guts in pain. "If you can call it lucky."

"So you embroidered the truth a bit. I can live with that."

"There's more. When we were on the road…"

"Go on."

"I made contact with Marshall."

"What are you talking about?"

"I wanted proof that he was going to pay me. I'd played ball with him—I left town, I told you the cover story and all the rest of it—but how did I know he'd keep his side of the bargain? He got what he wanted. I was out of the way, and you wouldn't let me talk to anyone. What if he just decided to cut me out? So I called him up and said I wanted money, or I'd go to the police and tell them about Trey Peters."

"How much did you ask for?"

"A hundred-thousand dollars."

I whistled.

"That kind of money means nothing to Marshall," said Jody. "He said Ferrari would deliver it as a gesture of goodwill."

"And instead, he sent someone to kill us, right. That night in Lincoln. You thought that guy was delivering the money?"

Jody said nothing for a while, just shrugged his shoulders and stared at his feet. He looked sick and old.

"You don't know what it's like to have nothing, Dan."

"Oh, yeah? Try me."

"A hundred-thousand dollars would get me out of New York. I could start again."

"As what? A masseur?"

He wiped his eye with the back of his hand. The tears looked real enough. "You can laugh if you want."

"I'm not laughing, Jody." I waited for him to stop crying. "So what happened?"

"You remember that gas station we stopped at—after the guy tried to shoot us?"

"Bill and Hank? I'm not likely to forget it."

"While you were filling the truck, I called Marshall again. This time the price had gone up."

"And he agreed?"

"Yes." Tears ran down Jody's face. "Two hundred grand. I could have started a new life with that."

No mention of me. He was only ever thinking of the money. I felt sick. "Go on."

"He asked me where we were headed, and I told him Buffalo. He wasn't happy about that, told me I should have stayed out of New York, and I knew he was scared. I said I'd go straight to the police and tell them he'd tried to have me killed if he didn't have the money waiting for me there." He sobbed and doubled over in pain, clutching his stomach. "And then they picked me up in that car."

I wanted to comfort him, but I couldn't. My hands lay like lead in my lap. We watched the traffic go by.

"When we got to that place in New Jersey, they took me into a room and said wait for Ferrari, he'd be there in a minute, and they locked the door. That was it. Nobody came. No food, nothing to drink, I had to piss in the corner of the room. It was cold. I couldn't hear anything. I shouted but nobody came. I thought they were going to leave me there to die. And I guess I realized that I'd made a mistake."

"At last."

"Marshall never meant to pay me. And the only good thing that had happened to me... Well, I screwed that up, didn't I?"

I didn't ask what he meant. I didn't want any more "I love you" bullshit. He may have loved my dick, but he loved money more. That's what he was thinking of all the time. I was just—what? Something to pass the time? A driver? A human dildo? Two hundred-thousand bucks was worth more than my stupid dreams of gold-enrod and joe-pye weed and dogs in the yard.

"Finally I heard noises; someone had turned up. I shouted and shouted till I lost my voice. Then Ferrari came."

I swallowed and felt tears prick my eyes. Whatever Jody had done, he didn't deserve what happened.

"I think he was drunk, or he was on GHB or something. He was crazy. I tried talking to him, I asked him for my money, and he started hitting me. He got my head and started beating it against the wall until I pretty much passed out. Then he...you know." Jody's voice dropped to a whisper. "He fucked me."

"He raped you."

"I don't know. I thought if I let him do it he might let me go. He might be nice to me." Jody put his face in his hands and started weeping. "God, he hurt me so much. And then... He took me to that room...where you were...and he made me..."

"I know." I put my arm around his shoulders. "I know what he did."

He cried like his heart was breaking. The day was turning cold, and he wasn't wearing enough. People were staring. "Come on," I said. "Let's get you home."

"Home." His voice wobbled. "Yeah."

And so we tottered slowly along the sidewalk, Jody leaning into me, sniffing heavily, occasionally groaning. I felt nothing—cold, empty, not even disappointed. Closed down. The dream that I'd chased out of New York had disappeared, just another mirage. Martin Kingston was a fool. The world didn't work the way he wanted it to. Repentant hookers didn't fall in love with battle-scarred loners. The ghosts of dead young marines didn't organize happy endings for the lovers they'd left behind. All we had was survival and the endless quest for money. Everything else was just dick in ass. Friction. Temporary relief from loneliness. Illusion.

I got Jody to bed.

"You tired?"

"Yeah."

"Think you can sleep?"

"Mmm-hmm."

Neither of us looked at the other.

"Okay. I'll just…" I didn't complete the sentence. I'll just what? Be downstairs? Fix us some food? Put up some more shelves, clean out some more cupboards? What for? I'll just get the first train out of here, don't care where. Steal a car or hitch a ride, hit the road until the road runs out.

I crept quietly down the stairs, as if silence would make it easier to leave.

And here the story might end. Two losers going their separate ways, like a million other losers every day. There was nothing to keep me in Ann Arbor. Steve could take care of Jody; there was no point in me hanging around doing my handyman act. I was an embarrassment to both of them. I didn't much like the idea of going back to New York. I'd pick up a few belongings from that flat in 109th Street, but there was no way I would ever live there again. I was finished with New York. Maybe I should do what Jody had done—pick up the threads of my life, see if there was any family left back in Massachusetts who had any use for an unemployed, disgraced ex-marine with a history of violence and a recent involvement with organized crime.

It was too late to think about going anywhere tonight. I still had enough money to check into a hotel; it would make a nice change from being eaten alive by the bugs that shared the sofa at Steve's place, no matter how much insecticide I sprayed. Maybe I'd find company in one of the bars, some student or factory worker who was willing to stick his legs in the air for me. It was a long time since I'd fucked anyone—and the last time, I was shot up with tranquilizers and being filmed by a psychotic gangster who then tried to kill me. That kind of thing could put a man off sex.

So why was I still walking up and down Main Street, talking to myself? Why wasn't I at the train station, buying a ticket? If I felt nothing, if my heart was dead, why was the damn thing beating so hard?

Because, damn it, fuck it, fuck it, *fuck it*, because I cared about Jody. It was nothing to do with what Martin had said, it was nothing to do with Will Laurence and what happened in Afghanistan; this was about me and Jody, Jody and me, and it was real and it hurt. It hurt because I wanted him and he didn't want me, I loved him and he didn't love me, all he wanted was his two hundred-grand and he'd forget all about us; I could go on pretending that it didn't matter and it wasn't happening, I could run back to New York and it would still hurt. I could get over it—of course I could, I'd got over worse. Wounds always heal, and I have so many scars that one more won't make much difference.

But this time, I didn't want to walk away. I didn't want to get over it. I wanted Jody so much—even if he'd lied to me and used me, even if he'd sold me down the river for a few thousand bucks and the lies that Marshall and Ferrari told him—I still felt the same way I felt when we were on the road, or when Martin was driving me up to Ann Arbor, when I was sitting by that hospital with Steve, waiting for Jody to come around.

I felt something. And whatever it was—love, disappointment, anger—was better than the big fat nothing that I'd have if I walked away now. Maybe we'd just fight, we'd say bitter things and I'd leave in even worse shape than I already was. Well, hell, someone would take me in. Martin, my family, someone. Wouldn't they?

And there would be others.

Yeah. There would be others. Better than this. Guys who didn't lie, who didn't steal and blackmail and deal drugs.

Come on, Dan. Get a train out of here, anywhere, fast. One foot in front of the other. Just keep walking.

But this isn't the way to the station. This is the way back to Steve's house, to the crummy neighborhood of row houses and trash cans and dog shit and bugs in the furniture.

This is the way back to Jody.

I walked up the street to the house and I rang the doorbell. It was nine o'clock in the evening. Maybe Steve would be home, maybe he wouldn't.

I rang, and nobody answered.

Walk away, Dan. Walk away now, before it gets worse.

But I stayed and I waited, and that is the hardest thing I have ever done. Harder than all the fighting and killing, harder than living a secret life, hiding the truth, harder than Will dying and all that followed.

I waited like a fool outside that house and there was nothing to protect me, no strategy, no back up, no rules. I was unarmed.

And finally, just as I was ready to turn around and walk away, I heard the uneven thump of footsteps descending the stairs, and Jody's voice, strained, distant, approaching.

"Dan? Is that you? Dan? Don't go away." Nearer. "Please don't go away. I'm coming, Dan. I'm coming as fast as I can."

The door opened, and he stood there thin, pale, sweating. He looked feverish.

"Oh, Jesus, Dan. I thought you'd gone."

I opened my arms and took hold of him, feeling the wetness of his hair, his forehead, as it stuck to my face.

"I thought you'd gone. I thought..."

I closed the door behind me. "It's okay," I said. "I'm here."

And I carried him upstairs to bed.

**James Lear** is the internationally bestselling author of gay erotic fiction, including *The Back Passage, The Palace of Varieties,* and *A Sticky End.* His novels regularly top the Amazon rankings, and in 2008 he was named Writer of the Year at the Erotic Awards. Mr. Lear lives and works in London. *The Hardest Thing* is his seventh novel.

The Bestselling Novels of James Lear

The Mitch Mitchell Mystery Series

The Back Passage
By James Lear

"Lear's lusty homage to the classic whodunit format (sorry, Agatha) is wonderfully witty, mordantly mysterious, and enthusiastically, unabashedly erotic!" —Richard Labonté, Book Marks, Q Syndicate
ISBN 978-1-57344-423-5 $13.95

The Secret Tunnel
By James Lear

"Lear's prose is vibrant and colourful...This isn't porn accompanied by a wahwah guitar, this is porn to the strains of Beethoven's *Ode to Joy*, each vividly realised ejaculation accompanied by a fanfare and the crashing of cymbals."—*Time Out London*
ISBN 978-1-57344-329-6 $15.95

A Sticky End
A Mitch Mitchell Mystery
By James Lear

To absolve his best friend and sometime lover from murder charges, Mitch races around London finding clues while bedding the many men eager to lend a hand— or more.
ISBN 978-1-57344-395-1 $14.95

The Low Road
By James Lear

Author James Lear expertly interweaves spies and counterspies, scheming servants and sadistic captains, tavern trysts and prison orgies into this delightfully erotic work.
ISBN 978-1-57344-364-7 $14.95

Hot Valley
By James Lear

"Lear's depiction of sweaty orgies...trumps his Southern war plot, making the violent history a mere inconsequential backdrop to all of Jack and Aaron's sticky mischief. Nice job." —*Bay Area Reporter*
ISBN 978-1-57344-279-4 $14.95

Ordering is easy! Call us toll free or fax us to place your MC/VISA order.
You can also mail the order form below with payment to:
Cleis Press, 2246 Sixth St., Berkeley, CA 94710.

ORDER FORM

QTY	TITLE	PRICE

SUBTOTAL _____

SHIPPING _____

SALES TAX _____

TOTAL _____

Add $3.95 postage/handling for the first book ordered and $1.00 for each additional book. Outside North America, please contact us for shipping rates. California residents add 9% sales tax. Payment in U.S. dollars only.

* Free book of equal or lesser value. Shipping and applicable sales tax extra.

Cleis Press • Phone: (800) 780-2279 • Fax: (510) 845-8001
orders@cleispress.com • www.cleispress.com
You'll find more great books on our website

Follow us on Twitter @cleispress • Friend/fan us on Facebook